I0623443

Love at First Night

Love at First Night

A COWBOY MOUNTAIN MAN / CURVY GIRL ROMANCE

ROUGH & READY COUNTRY
BOOK NINE

ENGRID EAVES

Copyright © 2024 by Engrid Eaves

All rights reserved.

No part of this book may be reproduced or used in any manner or by any electronic or mechanical means, including information storage and retrieval systems, without written permission from the author, except for the use of brief quotations in a book review.

Cover created using Canva Pro and Deposit Photos.

This is a work of fiction. Names, characters, places, and incidents either are the product of the author's imagination or are used fictitiously. Any resemblance to actual persons, living or dead, events, or locales is entirely coincidental.
www.engrideaves.com

Contents

Prologue

HAWK

"You have to trust me," I say in low tones, running my hand possessively over Roxy's thick black braid and leaning in so close our faces remain a few breathless inches apart. "I'll never let you down."

Staring at her shapely lips, every cell in my body longs to kiss her, and my heart feels like it will explode. But I've never gotten up the nerve to do it. The middle of the Ophir City Rodeo Arena sure as hell isn't the place to get bold.

Still, we're running out of time...

Behind us, Milton clears his throat, shooting me a warning glare. He's my best friend and a royal pain in the ass since I started crushing hard on his little sister this year. With graduation over and departure for the Navy looming, this competition is bittersweet for Roxy and me. It's our last together. Maybe that's why she's uncharacteristically hesitant to compete today. Maybe it's why I've pushed so hard for this last event.

Roxy nods, a strange uncertainty I only started noticing this year flooding her face. It confuses the hell out of me. But

1

her eyes round, large and innocent, like a spring fawn's, and she licks her lips saying, "I trust you."

I flash a lopsided grin, willing myself to be what she needs, when she needs it. Especially for this race. We've spent six summers together now, running wild and free between the expansive valleys of Rough & Ready Ranch and Three Nations Reservation, which abut each other on the ranch's southern edge. Roxy and her brother, Milton, live there with their paternal grandparents, the Harjos.

Grandpa Billy Harjo and my foster dad, Wyatt, sit in the stands side by side. I look up, waving their direction, and they nod in reply. Both served in Vietnam, and Billy relocated to Rough & Ready after the war on Wyatt's urging. A member of the Delaware tribe out of Oklahoma, Billy ended up falling for a Wa-She-Shu woman named, Dot, which is how he ended up at Three Nations.

Reminding myself everyone's watching, I give Roxy the most fraternal wink I can muster and thank Milton for his help warming up. He frowns, wishing us good luck in solemn tones.

The Harjos aren't huge fans of Roxy and me racing. After all, the Wa-She-Shu were never a horse tribe like my people, the Shoshone-Bannocks. And buddy pick-up can be a dangerous sport. Over the years, though, they've resigned themselves to it with plenty of encouragement from Dad. I know they'll breathe a sigh of relief once today's over. With how Roxy's acting lately, maybe she will, too.

The black-haired beauty's voice pulls me back from my thoughts. Wetting her lips with her pretty pink tongue, she asks, "And do you trust me, Hawk?"

"With my life," I reply with more emotion than I mean to. She knits her pretty brows. Now's not the time for getting sentimental. Jumping on the back of my mount, I encourage, "Let's show 'em how it's done, Nammichi."

I circle the Ophir City arena, preparing with the other competitors, and steeling my mind for one last win. The trophies glistening in my family's stables drive me on. Even more than for myself, though, I want this win for Roxy, to rekindle the confidence and fire in her eyes missing this past year. And, if I'm being honest, to plant a seed in her mind... until I return from the Navy.

At the drop of the flag, the roan gelding I ride, Major, rips out of the starting line like a rocket. At this distance, Roxy looks small and fragile as I tear down the straightaway towards her. But her body is lithe and ready, like a mountain lion's, to jump atop the mount behind me.

Gripping the horse with my legs and leaning towards her, I extend my left arm as we flip around towards the starting line. The strength of our arms and momentum of the turning horse should aid her in launching up into the saddle behind me. It requires supreme confidence and courage...

She grabs me at the elbow, swinging up. We've done this hundreds of times, and I anticipate the secure feel of her petite arms around my waist.

Only something goes wrong. She never makes it onto the horse, or maybe she slides off. Instead of holding me, her arms slip, and she slams into Major's flank, trying to gain momentum to vault back up. But she loses her balance, dragged beneath the horse's back hooves.

It happens so fast I have no time to react. The next instant, I turn the horse, galloping towards her, sprawled in the arena dirt. Jumping from the saddle, I cross the distance, sprinting to her side, anxious to ensure she's okay.

Tears pour down her cheeks, and she wails and rocks back and forth, gripping her contorted arm. My pulse pounds in my temple as I register the sickening sight of the bone sticking out near her wrist and angry pools of scarlet. I kneel in front of her, irrationally repeating, "I'm sorry. I'm so sorry."

I lean forward, but she shrinks away, screaming, "Don't touch me!"

Sitting back on my heels, I watch numbly as first responders race into the ring, assessing her shattered extremity and less visible injuries. I hear them communicating their observations in low tones as she wails—a soul-searing sound I'll remember until my dying day.

Every eye in the arena bores into me, branding me with recrimination. Something went wrong. I don't know what, and now Roxy's paying the price. I promised her: *I'll never let you down*. What a fucking stupid thing to say.

Milton reaches the spot where I kneel. Only instead of asking what happened, he hauls me up by the collar of my shirt to my feet, slamming his fist into my face. Under any other circumstances, I'd duck or block his punch, ready with an uppercut of my own. But now, I let him knock me backwards, stumbling to keep my balance.

Lunging forward, he grabs my shirt, waving his finger in my face and screaming, "I told you this would happen. You should've never encouraged her to race. I knew she'd end up hurt, and it's all your fault!"

He slams his fist into my face again, and the world momentarily darkens as my ears ring. I don't fight back, because his fury is nothing compared to the self-loathing and anger swelling inside of me. "Leave Roxy the fuck alone! I don't want to see you near her again. You understand?"

Staggering back for a second time and wiping blood from my eyes, my gaze falls on the paramedics who have my broken pick-up on a stretcher. Scattered audience applause fills the arena as they carry her towards the exit. Milton stalks behind, never looking back.

A sting of realization hits me. All this time, I thought I was an honorary part of the Harjo family. Milton and Roxy called me brother, and like a fool, I believed their words. Grandpa and Grandma Harjo welcomed me among the People, and I bought into their fucking lies. But Three Nations is no different than Dead Horse.

I'm unwanted and rejected by both. At Dead Horse, I was the castoff of a drunken one-night-stand, relegated to an early childhood of neglect and misery. Here, it's my own damn fault. But either way, it proves something I've known deep down my entire life. I don't belong anywhere, *with any people*. I just hope my Rough & Ready foster family never figures this out.

An hour later, Dad and I pull out of the rodeo arena parking lot. Still shaken to the core by everything that happened, I need to talk to my racing partner, to hear her voice and know she's okay.

"I want to see Roxy," I demand, staring incredulously at my Dad's chosen route. Instead of making the turn towards the hospital, we're headed back to the ranch. *What the fuck?*

The suntanned cowboy shakes his head, side-eyeing me inside the cab of my beat up 1967 Chevy pickup. He wouldn't let me drive, thanks to my emotional and mental state.

"The Harjos need some family time, son, and you need to cool your heels when it comes to that girl. Let things calm down for a bit. Emotions are running too high right now."

"But I need to be there for her. She's my pickup, and she's injured, and it's all my fault," I spit, rage rising in me. I haven't felt this tumult of emotions since coming to Rough & Ready in the first place. I thought I had better control of myself, but not being there for her kills me. "I have to see her with my own two eyes. Make sure she's okay."

He grits out, "She's not okay."

Deep down, I know this. After all, the images of the day won't stop looping in my mind. Still, some dumbass part of me clings to irrational optimism. Unable to process anything but anger, I punch the passenger door of my truck three times in quick succession, leaving a dent. Bam! Bam! Bam! Only after I see bruised and bleeding knuckles do I feel some relief.

Years of working with the worst of the worst foster boys means my last move doesn't phase Dad in the least. Calmly, he declares, "When the Harjos want to see us, they'll let us know."

"I've got to make sure she's okay, Dad. I can't leave things this way." Roxy's voice runs through my head. *Don't touch me.*

"Give them time, Hawk. Besides, it wouldn't hurt you to do a little calming down before you see her again."

"But I'm leaving for the Navy in three days. I've got to make things right with her before I go. Hell, I wanted to spend as much time..." I catch myself. "With the Harjos as I could before leaving."

Dad shoots a stern glare in my direction that makes me straighten up. "I already told you, son, fourteen and eighteen don't mix."

"I only turned eighteen two weeks ago," I observe morosely.

He shakes his head. "The law's the law, son." Under his breath, he continues, "Feels like we just went through this with Christian and Cricket. You boys need to finish growing before you start thinking about coupling. Y'all are multiplying the gray hairs on my head."

Guilt washes over me, followed by desperation. "I need to see her. I never meant to hurt her..." I can't finish the sentence. *Who cares what I did or didn't mean to do?* All that matters is she got hurt...bad.

The cowboy grumbles, "I know what you've got on your mind, and I'm putting my foot down. When the Harjos are ready, you can see her. Whether that happens before or after you leave for basic is out of our hands. But you *will* leave that girl alone until she's grown. You understand me?"

I don't even know what I have in mind with Roxy. How in

the hell can he? I just need to be with her before I leave. The reality of how much my life will change in a handful of days slams into me.

Things will never be the same again, and I can't do anything about it. Kind of like when I left Dead Horse Reservation and ended up in foster care here. Only that proved a more welcome relief than I could have possibly imagined. I have to hope something positive will come out of the change this time around, too. Nevertheless, my stomach churns as thoughts of Roxy clutching her arm run wild through my mind, putting a cold sweat on my forehead.

"Have you heard anything more from Billy?" I ask, sinking into the threadbare upholstery of the passenger seat, crossing my arms, and finally resigning myself to the immediate future I can't change.

He pinches the bridge of his nose for a moment before looking back at the road. "Last thing I heard she's heading into surgery for her arm. And doctors are observing her for a concussion."

Biting down hard on my lower lip, I fight back the tears clouding my eyes and sliding down my cheeks. I never wanted to hurt her. And we've performed that move countless times together. *How did it go so wrong?*

Another realization smacks me over the head. Roxy's the most precious thing in my world, and there's absolutely nothing I can do about it...*except let her go*. If she never wants to see me again, after what happened, how can I blame her?

My shoulders shudder, and my body tenses as I fight back a sob. Despite the long ebony sheets of hair hiding my face and emotions, Dad must sense my turmoil. He squeezes my shoulder with his left hand.

"Hawk, there's nothing you could have done differently. I watched the entire race. She lost her nerve, and her arms slipped. It was that simple."

I can't speak because of the tears pouring down my face—like a damn pussy. This type of display won't go over well in basic.

Swallowing loudly, I manage, "If I could change places with her, I'd do it in a heartbeat." I rub my hand over my chest, realizing that over the past six summers together, Roxy has become my heartbeat. Not knowing if she's okay, not being able to comfort her are torments matched only by my fear things will never be the same between me and her again.

Chapter One

HAWK

THIRTEEN YEARS LATER

"We need to talk about Roxanne..." Turner's voice trails off flatly, visually echoed by the white puffs his breath leaves in the early morning March air. The clean-shaven brunette custom home-builder brings his spirited buckskin gelding, Bugsy, alongside my mount, Checkers, a gentle Appaloosa mare.

First, LocalMatch and now this? My heart jumps in my chest. Sighing, I reply, "What's she done now?"

"How do I put this?" he thinks out loud. "I guess bluntly—"

I interrupt with a grumble, "Can't imagine it any other way from you, bro."

He rubs his stubbly chin for a moment. "Now, don't get me wrong. I appreciate her, and she's my favorite waitress at the Silver Fork since my wife no longer works there. But she came pretty damn close to breaking Lily and I up."

My eyebrows jump. "Seriously? How did she do that?"

"Well, she told Lily that I only married her to secure a business deal..." His voice trails off.

The facts surrounding my foster brother's rushed marriage one month ago remain a little jumbled in my mind. So, I ask, "Why did she say that?"

He shrugs. "Because she overheard a conversation between me and Broderick about joining our custom home design firms. Roxy heard him tell me he'd feel better about the deal if I settled down and tied the knot. You know, in keeping with his company's family home branding..."

I narrow my eyes, grimacing. "Well, did you or didn't you have that conversation?"

"We did," Turner growls. "And Roxanne did overhear it. But then she let her imagination run wild, and it became a huge thing."

"What do you mean by huge thing?" I don't mean to sound irritated, but my brother's accusation sounds lofty.

"She came up with this whole cockamamie idea that I roped Christian into helping me bring the full force of Child Protective Services down on Lily so that her five younger siblings would be taken away, and she'd have to marry me to get them back..."

His words elicit a sharp exhale from me. Christian is the sheriff of Gold County and honorable to the core. How Roxy could entertain such a notion about him, I can't comprehend.

"Why would she think that?" Turner's known Roxy nearly as long as I have, so she should be a better judge of his character, too. Then again, we all grew apart after the accident and my enlistment.

Turner sighs. "That's my point. Roxanne fabricated the idea out of an overheard conversation and her imagination. But it nearly destroyed my marriage."

"That girl." I groan. As much as I love the copper-skinned beauty who I've kept at arm's length ever since returning to

Rough & Ready a year and a half ago, I'm also well-acquainted with her faults. For one, she's impatient, rushing to judgment before gaining a full picture of what's going on.

"I don't know what pisses me off more, Hawk. The fact she actually thought Christian, me, and our family are capable of that kind of bullshit. Or how much her ridiculous theory nearly cost me. And to top it off, Lily's angry as a cornered rattlesnake. And you and I both know cornered rattlesnakes..."

"End up biting themselves," I finish with a perplexed frown. "So, why do you think Roxy took things so far?" I ask, uncertain I want to hear the answer.

"Hell if I know," Turner replies, shaking his head. "But what matters is Lily thinks Roxanne has a thing for me and was purposely trying to break us up, which has brought out a crazy jealous streak in my woman..."

"That's ridiculous," I mumble under my breath, my stomach sinking. *Roxy has a thing for Turner?* I rub the spot over my heart absentmindedly, thinking back to how that bubbly girl flirts with every man who walks into the Silver Fork. Every man except for me, of course...

"All I know is this town's too damn small to have Lily and Roxanne at each other's throats for the next twenty years."

"You think Lily would hold a grudge that long?" I ask skeptically.

"She's a redheaded Scorpio. Need I say more?" my brother replies. "If I even mention Roxanne's name, my woman turns bright red and stomps out of the room. It's a shame because, according to Lily, they really hit it off in the beginning. And the Harjos are like family. I want to be able to invite them to the wedding."

Even though Lily and Turner are married, they sent out save the date announcements recently for an official to-do in July. In that context, I'm not sure how I feel about his last sentence. Things have been awkward with the Harjos ever since that fateful last race. It even put a rift between Wyatt and Grandpa Billy, although Milton and I patched up our friendship in the service. Nevertheless, I can't ignore the fact fate seems to want to throw Roxy and I together these days.

"I'm not sure I'm the best person to talk to Roxy... And honestly, I'm avoiding her at the moment, thanks to LocalMatch."

Turner's eyebrows shoot up. "What about LocalMatch?"

"It damn well listed Roxy and I as ninety-eight percent compatible."

"Ninety-eight percent?" Turner chuckles.

I humph as if it's the most ridiculous thing ever. "I've been avoiding the Silver Fork ever since." I leave out the torment of not being able to get the off-limits Wa-She-Shu beauty off my mind. But then when hasn't it been this way?

To my surprise, Turner doesn't look shocked...at all. Instead, he says, "Wait, why?"

"Why? Are you crazy? You know the bad blood between the Harjos and our family since the accident. It took me years to patch things up with Milton. I don't want to fuck up our friendship by messing with his sister again."

Despite my words, I can't get the photos Roxy posted on her dating profile out of my head. They've been the catalyst for all sorts of dangerous and painful ruminations. Desires I thought I excised when I left Rough & Ready.

Ever since moving back, I've managed to ignore my childhood friend apart from seeing her at the Silver Fork. But her profile's opened up a Pandora's Box of repressed emotions that I'm not sure I can abide. Maybe I never should've come back. Maybe I should re-enlist...

My thoughts wander to those jaw-dropping, mouthwatering images, perfectly showcasing her generous curves and ample tits. All those womanly parts of her that filled out when

I was away serving my country. A red-and-black floral sundress with a cowgirl hat, a tight black dress with cowboy boots, accentuating her shapely legs, and a tight-fitting pair of Ariat jeans with a floral tank top. Fuck, I have to adjust how I'm sitting and gulp air, just thinking about it.

Turner's brows raise. "The bad blood you're referencing is all in your head, Hawk. You need to let the past go, quit feeling guilty over something you couldn't control. Besides, if we don't invite the Harjos to the wedding, we sure as hell will have fresh bad blood between us."

I shrug. "Then, invite them. How's it my problem?"

"It's not that simple. Lily and Roxanne have to make up first. Besides, with the way Roxanne looks at you when we dine at the Silver Fork, I'd wager you're the next brother coupling up. So, patching things up between our women will help you in the long run. That is, if you'd quit ignoring our childhood friend..."

"Leave Roxy the fuck alone," I growl before catching myself.

Turner laughs. "You forget. I'm a married man now. Got my hands way too full with a sassy redheaded artist to think about anyone else."

"Good thing."

My brother cocks his head at me. "Do I detect a hint of jealousy?"

"I thought it was bad enough when an algorithm suggested Roxy and me. But you should know better. I never date rez girls."

"Yeah, I've heard you say that once or twice. Honestly, seems a little hypocritical to cut out a whole segment of the population based on where they live."

I shake my head, frowning. "Rez girls lead to rez houses and rez lifestyles, and I want no part of that. Too much crime and poverty." *Too much never truly belonging, too.*

13

"Maybe at Dead Horse. But Three Nations doesn't seem half bad."

"Nope," I reply emphatically. "I've had my fill of reservations for a lifetime, even the fancy ones with casinos. Besides, didn't you hear about the woman who just went missing from Three Nations? Shelby Swiftwater. Her face is plastered everywhere. Shit like that happens all the time on reservations, and law enforcement never seems to get to the bottom of it. I'd never want to be married or raise daughters in that kind of place."

Turner takes a deep breath, shaking his head. "That's just like you, Hawk. No prospects of settling down, yet you're worrying about a fictitious wife and daughters..."

"Planning ahead is how I got where I am today." Diverting my eyes towards the blue of the Sierra Nevada Mountains, white-capped with snow, I savor the warmer than usual March temperatures. "And that includes *not* dating Roxy."

He continues, "All I know is you two racing together was a breathtaking sight."

"That was a long time ago."

"Might've been but when it comes to your current trajectory with women, what you're doing isn't working. Maybe it's time to try a different tack—"

"Not if that tack involves my best friend's little sister..."

"Whatever you say," Turner replies, looking thoroughly unconvinced.

We ride in silence for a spell. *Thank goodness!* Finally, I get the morning I came out here seeking. My eyes sweep the majestic, untamed beauty of the ranch, teeming with the sounds of raucous morning songbirds and the bubbling chatter of the brook we follow. I need this time to ground myself, draw closer to nature before my day gets hectic with emergency flights. I have contracts with the hospital, search and rescue, and the fire department. It can make for insane work hours, day and night.

Nearing the end of our ride, Turner asks again, "You think you can help patch Lily and Roxanne's relationship back up?"

I shake my head, frowning. "After what you just described? There's no way in hell I'm wading into the middle of that..."

"You and I both know you've got extra pull with her, Hawk. So, I'm calling in a favor."

I shake my head, my blood simmering. "*Had* extra pull with her. More than a decade ago. Besides, according to Lily, you're the one with influence over Roxy now. Instead of bossing me around like one of your subcontractors, maybe you should sort this out yourself."

"Lily would kill me," he spits back.

"Good riddance," I mutter under my breath.

"What?"

"Nothing." Looking up at the periwinkle sky, I lament, "I knew I should have gone riding alone today." That decision would have kept me from feeling *this feeling* whatever the hell it is...

Annoyance? Anger? Jealousy. Ah, hell no. I refuse to acknowledge that rogue emotion.

"Please. Once Lily and Roxanne are back to being friends, trust me, it'll be better for both of us."

"It will have no effect on me whatsoever," I reply through gritted teeth.

"Sure," my brother laughs heartily. "Look, I'm not about to beat a dead horse, Hawk, and I know how stubborn you can be. Especially when it comes to your damn feelings. But one of these days you're going to thank me for this conversation... That is, if you agree to help me out."

I shake my head firmly, pulling off my cowboy hat and scratching my buzz cut head. "Consider me out."

Silence.

To prove my point, I add, "I'm probably meeting up with Crystal this weekend for drinks, anyway. You know the Truckee ski instructor I told you about a while ago?"

I haven't spoken with Crystal in three or four months. But she's always up for a couple of drinks, and I need to get off the subject of Roxy for good. I make a mental note to text her after my ride.

"Wait, do you mean the crazy blonde who reads Indian romances like they're going out of style and insists on calling you Geronimo in the bedroom?"

I scrunch my face, regretting I ever told him about that. "Crazy Horse... not Geronimo. And it's a size thing...not because I'm Native."

Turner lifts an eyebrow.

"You know, hung like a—"

He roars with laughter, cutting me off. "It's a Native thing. Trust me."

Shaking my head, I add, "I didn't say I want to spend the rest of my life with her or anything. But the sex isn't bad."

"I thought you were looking for more than a bootie call. Besides, with the right woman, the sex is fucking mind-blowing." Eyeing me critically, Turner counters, "Crystal's using you for your skin color. Sounds like objectification to me."

"And what do you know about objectification?"

"Plenty. Whether it's cowboys or Indians, lots of women treat us like walking stereotypes. A notch in the bed frame—"

I interrupt, "Isn't that another stereotype?"

Ignoring me, he continues, "Add in the millionaire factor, and I was surrounded by women who wanted me for all the wrong reasons...until I met Lily." He laughs, smacking his hand on his thigh, and I roll my eyes. *Do I really have to hear this again?* "That woman wanted nothing to do with my hat, boots, buckle, or bank account."

"What do you have left?" I tease. "Don't tell me she fell for your personality..."

"She sure did."

"Poor girl—"

"Hawk, she's my soulmate and twin flame."

More of that New Age shit he keeps spouting since getting married. "You can take the boy out of the hippie commune, but you can't take the hippie out of the boy..."

"I'm serious," Turner interjects with a firm nod. "But who am I to talk? Let me know how the Geronimo thing works out for you."

"Crazy Horse..."

We take off across the meadow at breakneck speed, shrouded in the golden light of early morning and juxtaposed against a towering backdrop of Sierra Nevada peaks.

"Whoever reaches the barn first talks to Roxanne," Turner challenges with a grimace, leaning into his mount.

"Deal!" I shout, urging Checkers on. I knew I should've tacked up that nimble, new Arabian this morning...

Chapter Two

Mrs. McCreary shoots a dour smile my direction. "I specifically said no cantaloupe in my side of fruit. Take it back to the kitchen." She pushes her entire plate towards me, and my jaw drops. She may be unhappy with the side, but the rest of the plate is perfect. Talk about a waste of good food!

The standing order at the Silver Fork is never to argue with Mrs. McCreary, an older woman who takes pride in being the most difficult customer in Hollister.

I worry my lower lip, trying hard to follow the rules. But I'm already four hours into an exhausting shift, and the door has just rung behind me letting me know I have another guest. I call over my shoulder without even looking, "Please seat yourself. I'll be with you in a minute."

I've spent the last month listening to self-help books to combat the insecurity that's plagued me since high school when my body started changing. I'm working on developing leading lady energy like my former friend, Lily. We may not be talking these days, but Lily still taught me a ton about the value of confidence and assertiveness.

18

Besides, if that curvy girl could nab a hunk like Turner West, it's time I start loving myself and my body. Of course, the unwanted side effect of my recent work, affirmations, and journaling is a forthright way of speaking and setting boundaries that not everyone appreciates. I can feel this newfound attitude bubbling towards the surface, even as I strain to repress it.

Sighing loudly and staring at the elderly woman, I reply, "Cantaloupe, oranges, and grapes are it for the day...as I told you when you ordered."

Her face falls, and I wait for lightning to strike me dead for breaking the house rules. Fortunately, Zeus appears to be off duty.

"I would like to speak with your manager," she replies, her tone biting.

I swallow nervously. Nervous because I've reached my breaking point, and I can no longer hold back the torrent of words that follow. "The only manager is Jerry, and he's in the back cooking his patootie off...and adding cantaloupe to the fruit. So, unless you'd like to talk to him, I suggest diving into your otherwise fine plate of food while I head into the kitchen to replace your side with...what? Toast?"

She frowns, taken aback by my matter-of-fact response. Yes, my words sound snippy, but I work hard, I mean really hard, to keep my tone even and my face calm and smiling.

"Toast. But not too crisp."

"White, sourdough, or English muffin?"

"English muffin. Oh, and be a dear and please bring me more of the marmalade."

I swallow hard, squeezing the serving tray I hold with both hands. Through gritted teeth, I remind her, "We're out of marmalade until the next shipment comes in."

"This is becoming intolerable," the old lady replies.

I raise my eyebrow in full agreement.

"In that case, blackberry," she hisses. "Oh, and I could use a warm up on my coffee."

"Of course." As I walk away, I can't help but curse my current situation. Lily barely started working here before she bailed to marry Turner, Hollister's millionaire custom home-builder. I can't blame her.

After that, Jerry hired a gal named Shelby from Three Nations to serve with me. We even carpooled together some mornings. Carpooled enough for me to learn about some of the demons she struggled with, like her abusive, controlling boyfriend. I'm guessing that's why she went AWOL. Like police-are-searching-for-her AWOL. I hope the poor thing's alright.

Present circumstances mean I pull double duty until further notice, because finding good employees in a town of two thousand residents is no simple task. As for me, the pay's the same despite double the work. It makes the effort utterly thankless, apart from extra tips.

Straightening my back and raising my chin defiantly, I start towards the kitchen when a strong hand reaches out, grabbing my wrist. Startled I turn, staring at my brother's best friend, Hawk Daggett. He sits at one of the black-painted, dark-green upholstered booths, punctuated by dark wood flooring and brick walls.

From his tanned skin and muscular frame to his high cheekbones and soulful mahogany eyes, he takes my breath away. And the hand that grasps my arm sends delicious sparks of electric lust straight to my heart, leaving me so flushed and breathless I can barely look him in the eyes. He's been home from the service for more than a year now, barely looking my way or saying a word to me beyond his order from the Silver Fork menu. So, the feel of his flesh on mine is unexpected and gratifying.

"Nammichi, you look overworked," he grumbles in soft-spoken, masculine tones. I'd love to read more into the warm concern flooding his face and the hand that slides the distance to clasp mine, squeezing my fingers. But I can't, thanks to the endearment he uses. *Nammichi*. Little sister. That's all I'll ever be to him... When he's not busy ignoring me.

"I am," I nod, breathing hard, and reluctantly pulling my hand away. I know better than to play with fire, especially flames kindled by an excruciatingly gorgeous Shoshone-Bannock helicopter pilot...

He frowns, holding up his menu. "I'm not sure what I want. But I do have plenty of questions. Might as well have a seat while I take a look."

"I can't possibly," I reply, exasperated. "Besides, you and I both know exactly what you're going to order. The steak and eggs over easy with a side of sourdough toast and a small orange juice."

He nods, motioning with his hand for me to sit down across from him.

Shaking my head, I whisper, "I can't, Hawk. I'm serving the whole diner right now."

"What happened to the customer is always right?" he asks with a dead-pan face.

"Hawk—"

"Sit down," he commands with older brother authority. I settle into the squeaky vinyl booth with a moan as the sudden lack of pressure on my feet confirms the awful intensity of their throbbing.

"Are you okay?" he asks, an amused smile lighting up his face at my display of pained ecstasy.

"Yeah, my feet are just killing me."

Reaching across the table, he grabs my right forearm, tracing his thumb over the scar where I had a compound fracture before my sophomore year of high school. His brows furrow, and I know exactly what he's thinking.

I observe firmly, "It wasn't your fault, you know."

He frowns, letting his disbelief-filled gaze meet mine. "Jerry's working you to the bone, Roxy. When's the last time you took a break?"

"A break?" I laugh. "What's that?"

"It's decided then. You're taking one now."

Before I can protest, Mrs. McCreary's nasally voice snakes its way to my ears. "Roxy, dear, I hope you haven't forgotten about my jam and toast?"

I start to get back up, but Hawk stops me, his hand still holding my arm. "Stay right there. I'll handle this."

My jaw hits the floor as I watch him jump up and swagger towards Mrs. McCreary's table. From his broad, well-defined shoulders to his tapered waist and muscular ass, he's a sight to behold in a tight black T-shirt from his Army National Guard unit that reads "Stealing from the Reaper" on the back. My greedy eyes sweep to his form-fitting Wranglers, one of his many bronc-busting belt buckles, and Spanish leather boots. His brown Stetson sits on the diner table next to my right arm.

He keeps his black hair buzzed military-style, filling me with nostalgia for the long, thick ebony locks of his youth. But I learned after he came home not to mention growing out his hair. As he disdainfully put it, the request proved I was "too rez."

The old woman's eyes light up with the same appreciation coursing through my veins as Hawk politely offers, "Roxy hasn't had her morning break yet. But I can bring you whatever you need."

She swallows hard, her eyes sweeping him from head to toe. Her cheeks flush, and she smiles sweetly, saying, "Well, aren't you a dear, worrying about our sweet little Roxy. Of course, she needs her break. I'll be fine until she's done."

"No, ma'am," he counters, pointing at her mug. "More coffee? And that was an English muffin with blackberry jam, right?" He winks, sending her hand reflexively to her heart.

I squeeze my eyes shut, waiting for Mrs. McCreary to accuse him of eavesdropping on our previous conversation. But to my utter amazement, she nods, thanking him profusely. I can't help but laugh to myself. Beneath all her bluster and bickering is a hotblooded woman who appreciates a good-looking Native cowboy as much as the next gal.

As he strides past the booth, I hiss, "What are you going to tell, Jerry?"

He turns, shrugging. "The truth. You need a break. And he's going to give it to you."

Jerry is linebacker sized with a New York accent and an imposing head chef attitude. Nobody talks to him this way. But none of these things phase Hawk—a rescue racer, bronc buster, and combat-tested helicopter pilot. *Oh, to be a fly on the kitchen wall!* I just hope I won't pay for it later, after Hawk leaves.

Minutes pass before he returns with a pot of coffee, topping off Mrs. McCreary's mug and delivering her toast with jam. After checking in with a couple other booths and letting everyone know I'm on break, he heads my direction, pouring me a cup of coffee before sitting back down. He meets my stunned expression with a firm nod, the corners of his mouth slightly turned down. "Alright, your fifteen begins now." He looks at his watch for good measure.

"Thank you," I manage, swallowing the lump that his presence puts in my throat. After more than a year home, why is he paying me attention now? Then, it hits me. The affirmations and self-help must be working. I sit up straight, smiling confidently.

Leading lady energy, Roxy. Leading lady energy...

Wrapping my hands around the mug he just poured, I

savor its warmth while letting my gaze unrepentantly devour him.

He shrugs. "Piece of cake."

Silence shrouds the booth as he returns the favor, staring at my face until my cheeks burn and the air sizzles between us. I can't look away. It would be too obvious, and yet focusing on his drool-worthy face and kissable mouth means a special kind of torture.

My heart booms in my chest, and I'm sure the entire restaurant can hear it. I swallow loudly, my breath coming faster, as I watch him lick his full lips.

"Roxy, give me your foot," he commands.

"Give you my what?"

"Your foot," he says impatiently.

I shake my head, not understanding what he means. *Leading lady energy.* I bring my foot tentatively up towards him beneath the table.

Impatiently, he grabs it, setting it in his lap and slipping my Mary Jane off. I clear my throat, trying *not* to focus on the feel of his thick, muscular thighs on the back of my calf and heel or the fact my foot sits perched mere inches from his cock. It's a lost cause.

Because of the height of the table, he angles my foot, massaging it expertly with his large, warm fingers as I try to suppress the ecstatic moan the unexpected move elicits. Thank goodness I showered before work and put on one of those delish smelling lotions from the mall in Ophir City. I surrender to the exquisite feel of his strong hands, kneading the strain and stress out of my sole.

What else could those gifted hands do?

"Is that good?" he asks, a dark, sensual edge to his voice.

Nodding, I press my lips tightly together to suppress the cries of pleasure his fingers try to tease out of me. His familiar touch takes me back to our childhood and the easy affection we once shared. Holding hands, braiding each other's hair, hugging, and rubbing noses for Eskimo kisses. Only this is far more delectable.

My eyes roll back in my head, and I close them again, enjoying the fugitive moment and attempting to ignore the urgent tension building at the top of my legs. It's another lost cause. When I open them again, staring across the table, his cheeks look darker and his eyes dangerously heated.

His expression takes me back to the Ophir City Rodeo Arena all those years ago and the command he gave before our race: *You have to trust me.* Despite the passage of time and how little attention he's paid me, a part of me buried deep down inside still trusts and loves him completely...though he's done nothing to deserve it for years now.

Clearing his throat, he commands, "Your other foot." I draw back the left one carefully, and he pulls the right into his lap. Removing my shoe, he begins the same process.

Every point where my body touches his or his flesh touches mine is pure incineration. *Does he know what he's doing to me?* His face is frustratingly unreadable.

Swallowing loudly, I say, "You keep spoiling me like this, and I might want to see more of you."

He frowns, kneading the sole of my aching foot until I shiver with pleasure. "What about Turner?"

"I don't know. What about him?"

His hands still, and he stares long and hard at my face. His own looks cut from impassive marble. "You'd get tired of me before you knew it."

I raise an eyebrow. "I doubt that. You seriously have no idea how much I needed this today."

"One look at you when I walked in the diner," he replies darkly. "And I knew exactly what you needed."

"And what do you need?" I ask breathlessly before catching myself.

25

Hawk shakes his head, licking his generous lips slowly, and I melt into the booth. My mind wanders, imagining what those soft lips and velvety tongue would feel like on other parts of my body.

His gruff voice pulls me back from the indecent reverie. "*We* need to talk."

Chapter Three

ROXY

Hawk's hands continue to massage me beneath the table, playfully raking his fingertips over the sole of my foot every now and again, tickling me and making it impossible to think.

What in the hell is going on? I nod, certain my voice will fail if I try to use it.

Silence.

I raise an eyebrow, encouraging him to speak.

He clears his throat, but nothing comes out.

My eyes narrow, and I croak, "Here or outside?"

"Here," he says quietly as his fingertips whisper over the flesh of my inner ankle and lower calf.

Letting out a long sigh, I notice a glimmer of satisfaction illuminate his face. He's getting something out of this exquisite torment.

But why? And what does it mean?

"Alright..."

He swallows hard and clears his throat again, going back to squeezing and caressing the tension from my sole. "I'm here to discuss what happened between you, Lily, and Turner."

I sigh, letting my head fall. *Really? That's why he's here?* I should have known it had nothing to do with my newfound confidence. "Lily sent you to talk to me?"

"No, Turner did."

"Okay..." I reply, exasperated.

"Are you going to explain what in the hell you were thinking?" His hands grip my foot beneath the table, unmoving.

I raise my palms, shrugging. "What's there to say? I jumped to a conclusion I shouldn't have, and I'm really sorry about it."

"But you nearly broke Turner and Lily up," he growls, setting my blood on fire and transforming the tension at the top of my legs into a painful throb. *Damn him and his gorgeous face and voice!*

"I didn't mean to. I was trying to look out for her, but I made a mistake. A big one."

"No, you were trying to break them up."

Shaking my head, I retort, "Now, why would I want to do something like that?"

His eyes narrow, and his face tightens. "You and I both know why."

I shake my head. "Oh my God, Hawk. No, I don't know why you think I'd do—"

"Because you have a thing for Turner," he spits. I sense and hear a raw edge to his voice that I don't understand.

"A thing for Turner?" I repeat with a laugh.

He nods firmly, his eyes flashing a challenge.

"There's no way." Angrily, I try to pull my foot away from him, but he won't let me.

"Don't lie to me, Roxy."

I grimace, frustrated by his accusation and the strength of his effortless grip. "He's cute and all but not really my type. Too uptight."

A muscle bounces in Hawk's jaw, and I can hear his teeth grind together. "He's less uptight than me."

I shake my head, confused by the comparison. But then, a strange realization slams into me. "Wait, are you jealous?"

"Just because LocalMatch ranked us highly compatible doesn't mean a thing," he replies too quickly.

My jaw hits the ground. *Is this why he's suddenly acting so funny?* "LocalMatch? What?"

"Yes, your profile got suggested to me a couple of days ago... Don't try to pretend you didn't see it."

I scowl, thinking out loud. "I can't remember the last time I checked LocalMatch..."

"Whatever. It doesn't mean anything anyway," he finishes sternly. "But you do need to change your pictures."

"Change my pictures? Why?" I ask, scrutinizing his stoic expression. Fresh waves of frustration wash over me.

"Because they're too... They make men think bad thoughts, Roxy. Thoughts your big brothers don't want other men thinking about you."

I raise a challenging eyebrow, thoroughly confused and intrigued by the conversation. "I don't mean to get technical, but I only have one older brother..."

He growls, "You know what I mean."

"No, I'm not sure that I do," I reply honestly.

"It doesn't matter anyway... You know, us getting paired online."

He's back on the LocalMatch thing? I have never wanted to read a mind more in my entire life. I nod, drowning in a sea of equal parts pleasure and bewilderment. Teasingly, I say, "I guess you're right. After all, I'm way too rez for you."

"That's right," he nods. But his eyes search mine with a strange urgency I don't understand.

"I mean, I still listen to XIT's 'Plight of the Redman,'" I tease, and he closes his eyes, shaking his head.

Training his gaze on me, he adds, "On cassette?"

"Is there any other way?"

A deep rumble comes from his chest. After all these years, I've made my former racing partner laugh. I feel vindicated and even more aroused, if that's possible. His unguarded chuckle has to be one of the sexiest sounds on the planet.

My right foot remains a tantalizing few inches away from his dick, making my head twirl. A gentle nudge of my foot, a return of the massaging favor, and Hawk will know exactly how little I think of him as an older brother. This may be my one shot...

But what if my attentions prove unwanted? I'll never hear the end of it...*for the rest of my life*. After all, the small-town grapevine has nothing on the reservation rumor mill.

Desperate for release, I fall back on humor to diffuse the thick tension. "Yeah, I'm way too rez for you. I use evaporated milk instead of creamer." Brainstorming the worst stereotypes I can muster about Indian reservation inhabitants, I continue, "I know exactly how far I can get after the empty light comes on in my car, and I use slices of white bread in place of hamburger buns. Isn't that how the jokes go?"

"Hot dog buns." He clears his throat, feathering his fingertips over my calf. "I'm surprised you've gone so refined. I thought for sure you'd use fry bread."

"Mmm...fry bread hamburger buns. Now, I need to try that," I whisper, feeling my cheeks burn. "Honestly, I shouldn't be talking to you right now because you have yet to make any effort to grow out your hair. And the last time I saw you at a powwow was more or less never."

"That's not true, Roxy. I went to one in middle school."

I frown. "That was a long time ago, and you were another person back then."

Sadness crosses his face, and I hold my breath, waiting for him to confide in me what's really going on. I should know better. I'm the last person on Earth he'd trust with anything. Hell, the only time I ever see him is when he comes into the diner to eat or on a date with yet another skinny blonde. He couldn't make it more clear through his actions or taste in women that I mean nothing to him.

To break the awkwardness, I fall back on the funny fat girl routine I've perfected since high school, teasing, "Don't even get me started on little sisters..."

He smiles sexily.

What in the hell is this cowboy trying to do? Leading lady energy, Roxy. Set firm boundaries. And whatever you do, don't let him make your panties melt...

Too damn late for that...

Pulling my phone out of my apron pocket, I check the time. "It's been nice talking to you, Hawk. Long time no see. And the foot massage was... Well, there are no words for that foot massage. But I need to get back to work. I suppose you want me to apologize to Lily?"

He hesitates. "I'd like to see you two try to smooth your differences out, considering how small Hollister is."

"She'll likely never see me again if she doesn't come in here," I argue, pointing out the obvious. "I can't imagine her hanging out at Three Nations, unless she's suddenly developed a gambling or smoking habit I don't know about."

"You need to get along," he says curtly.

"Why?"

He shrugs. "You might find yourself at the ranch sometime. No reason to make it awkward."

I laugh, knitting my brows together. *I haven't been to Rough & Ready Ranch in thirteen years. What would bring me there now?* Sarcastically, I tease, "And she and Turner could end up at the Red Dress Powwow, right? I know it's a helluva lot more likely than me seeing you there."

"It's not my thing," he growls. "Neither are the crowds that come with it."

"But it's a part of who you are, whether or not you want to admit it."

He shakes his head.

My heart softens as I stare at his handsome face, almost unable to pull my eyes away. I see in his stunning expression, beneath the layers of masculinity and discipline, the pain and insecurity that has marked him since the first time I laid eyes on him.

It's why he doesn't like reservations, even though he's loath to admit it. They take him back to his childhood and the horrible life of neglect and abuse he lived before going into foster care. Over the years, through snippets of conversation and half-told stories, I've pieced this together, although we've never discussed it explicitly. But it feels like a great, beating hole inside of him, keeping him from ever truly embracing the wholeness or completeness of being one of the People.

Never one to hide my feelings, I confess, "You know I'll do anything for you, Hawk. I'll talk to Lily and try to make things better."

Taking a deep breath, he commands on an exhale, "Come to their wedding with me."

"What?" I shake my head, confused. *Did I hear him right?*

"Come to their wedding with me," he repeats softly.

"Turner and Lily's wedding? Have they even set a date yet?"

He rubs his hand over his close-cropped scalp. "Yeah, they sent out save the date magnets last week. Sometime in July, I can't remember the exact day, but I'll get back to you. That is, if you'll go with me?"

"I wasn't invited for obvious reasons."

"But I'm inviting you now... And Grandpa Harjo, too."

I frown. *Is he inviting me as his date or as a guest of the family?* I state the obvious, "Whether I go will depend on what happens between Lily and me. I don't want to do anything to upset her and Turner's special day...especially after how I almost messed things up."

His eyes narrow, and I swear I see a hint of disappointment. He opens his mouth, hesitating for a moment before asking, "You still haven't explained why you did it, Roxy. Why you tried to convince Lily to break up with Turner."

My cheeks burn. Hawk is literally the last man on the face of the Earth I want to explain this to because it involves listing some of my greatest body hangups.

I frown, pressing my lips tightly together. "I know my break's got to be over..."

"Roxy," he orders. "Were you jealous of Lily?"

"If you must know, yes, I was," I say, looking away. "But that's not why I warned her."

The corners of Hawk's mouth turn down. "So, you do have a thing for Turner?"

Back to this again? I shake my head, wondering why I don't just save my breath. "No, jealous because she found a man and got in a relationship. That doesn't usually happen to girls like her and me. I mean, like ever."

"Girls like Lily and you? What do you mean?"

I glance at my phone, and my heart sinks. "Time's up. I have to get back to work." I'll probably never share another moment like this with Hawk again.

"Nammichi—"

Frustration flares at the sound of his endearment. It feels like an insurmountable wall separating us. *How will I ever get him to see me as anything other than a little sister?* I doubt I'll ever have another shot. Mustering every ounce of my new leading lady energy, I pull my best Sharon Stone or Angelina Jolie move.

Instead of withdrawing my right leg carefully, the way I

did with my left, I bring it forward, massaging my toes and foot into the zipper of his Wranglers. Lingering for a tantalizing moment, with just enough pressure to feel the firmness behind his fly. The physical reality proves his foot massage was more than brotherly.

I scold in a tone so seductive I don't know where it comes from, "I'm not your little sister."

His jaw hits the floor as I find my Mary Janes under the table, slipping them back on. I glide out of the booth and glance over my shoulder with a wink. "Your usual steak and eggs?"

He looks stunned for an awkward moment, and then he slides out of the booth. My cheeks burn as I catch a well-endowed eyeful before he adjusts his tight-fitting jeans.

Hawk's eyes sear me, letting me know he caught me staring at his package. Grabbing his Stetson, he places it atop his head, gruffly excusing, "Raincheck on breakfast." He tips his brown hat curtly and turns, striding towards the diner entrance.

I hold my breath, admiring his tight ass on the way out. That was it. My one chance to let Hawk know my feelings for him run much deeper than fraternal affection.

Watching him swagger across the parking lot and climb into his lifted white Ford F-250 without a solitary glance backwards, realization clobbers me. I may finally be embodying leading lady energy, but that doesn't mean Hawk will ever be my leading man.

Chapter Four

HAWK

After pulling out of the Silver Fork parking lot, I stop at the gas station, sitting in my truck and trying desperately to clear my mind.

All I can think about is the swipe of a foot. A simple yet brazen move that has my insides in knots and my cock on high alert.

Roxy doesn't know what she's done...

Trying to clear my mind, I grab my cellphone, staring at my recent notifications. Crystal's number lights up the screen. I texted her after my morning ride, and she replied back while I sat at the Silver Fork.

I'm sure to have a decent enough time with her. And it's not like she expects anything from me apart from a couple of drinks and a roll in the hay...

But fuck... I'm back to those petite little feet, and the look of pleasure that washed over Roxy's face when I massaged her. *What my fingers and hands could do to the rest of her!*

I still feel the surprise pleasure of the ball of her foot and toes pressing into my semi, which went insta-hard at her touch.

And that seductive smile and wink over her shoulder in my direction? I wanted to carry her back to my cabin...lay claim to those generous curves and that tempting softness once and for all.

I want her bad. I always have. But I had my feelings in check...until those damn profile photos. Add Roxy's flirtatious foot into the mix, and I'm a fucking train wreck. A train wreck hellbent on plowing into my childhood friend. The feel of her warm skin lingers on my flesh. The smoothness of her legs and the softness of her curves, compelling me to touch and caress her.

I can't give into these temptations. After all, there's no amount of lust on this planet that would make me do anything that risks hurting Roxy. And who the hell am I to assume Roxy would have me, anyway? Yes, the foot was highly flirtatious. But it could be little more than a one-off. Something to laugh about with her friends later. After all, I've never pretended to understand women.

Girls like her and me... My mind wanders back to questions raised by our conversation. *What does she mean?* I can't think of anything her and Lily have in common except for having worked at the same diner...*and Turner*. I clench my teeth together, anger tensing my whole body.

Why the fuck does the thought of Roxy and Turner make me so goddamn angry? Or honestly, the thought of Roxy with any man?

Her outgoing personality and unmatched bravery have always captivated me. I remember galloping bareback and bridle-less across the expansive meadows of Rough & Ready with her, Milton, and my foster brothers.

I've missed the impetuous daredevil version of Roxy I knew as a kid. Haven't seen her in years...only for her to re-emerge today through her naughty flirtation. A few more glimpses of that, and I'm a fucking goner.

Shit...

Rogue thoughts crowd my mind. Thoughts I haven't let myself entertain since I was eighteen...

I imagine drawing Roxy into my arms with a possessive growl and claiming her silky lips and hot, wet mouth. Her arms snake around my neck, drawing my hard chest against her generous breasts and fanning the intensity of the fire building deep in my core...

I let out a pained sigh. Now that the door of my mind is cracked, possibilities topple over themselves, filling me with a need that makes my cock throb as painfully as it did in the Silver Fork.

Roxy's naked skin pressed against mine, her hot breath panting in my ear as I push her over the edge... A thick knot of desire lodges in my throat. My lips are on her tits, feathering them with kisses before I suck her brown nipples, one at a time, into my mouth, teasing her with my teeth and tongue.

My head dips between her thick thighs, savoring her slick arousal and making her tremble and moan with every flick and whirl of my tongue. Would she taste as good as she smells?

Truth be told, I want to please the hell out of her. Rubbing her feet earlier, caressing her skin and tickling her... Fuck, my mind's filled with images of her ecstatic face. I can still smell her honeysuckle lotion on my hands. The options are endless when it comes to the pleasure I could bring to the rest of her body...

I know what I need to do. Turning the key in the ignition, the truck comes to life as I use my hands-free setup to call Milton. I've got to nip this in the bud...once and for all.

Although I chose to leave the service after four years in the Navy and eight more with the Army National Guard while attending Embry-Riddle, Milton opted to stay in with the aim of retirement. He's currently deployed, which makes the sound of his voice startling. I thought for sure my call would go straight to voicemail.

He exclaims, "Motherfucker! How the hell have you been?"

The happiness in his voice makes me feel like a lowlife. After all, just moments ago, I fantasized about fucking his little sister...

"I'm good, man. How about you?" I ask.

"Living the dream... What are you up to today?"

I answer honestly. "Just visited your sister at the Silver Fork. She's causing trouble as always."

He clears his throat. "What's she done now?"

"Spread rumors that made trouble between Turner and his wife."

"That's right. Turner's married now. How the hell did that happen?"

I rub my hand over my hair. "It's a long story..."

"Better save it for another day then... I've got to go in a sec. Sorry about my sis. What got her involved in Turner's marriage in the first place?"

I say through clenched teeth, "Turner says Roxy's got a crush on him—"

"No way," he replies resolutely.

"What do you mean 'no way'?"

"Is there any other way to say it? No way, man. Roxy most definitely does not have a thing for him."

"Mmm hmm," I grumble.

"Sorry about all that, though. You'll have to explain everything that happened to me later. And let me know if I need to step in..."

"Yeah, it's more or less sorted out now. It involved a misunderstanding of sorts. But you know how she runs her mouth sometimes."

"Believe me, I do."

I shake my head, even though I know he can't see the gesture. "It's all good. Like I said, we've more or less straightened it out now."

"Glad to hear it. You know how she gets when that imagination of hers goes into overdrive."

"Yep," I agree.

"I've got to give her a call to see how Grandpa's doing. Just been very busy these past few weeks."

I forgot to ask Roxy about Grandpa Harjo this morning. Another wave of guilt slams into me. That's what I get for thinking with my cock instead of my brain.

Milton asks, "But she's doing okay otherwise?"

"Seems like it... You won't believe the crazy shit that happened the other day, though..."

"Try me."

"LocalMatch rated her and me as highly compatible."

"Hmm...really?" Milton delivers the words in a laidback tone that catches me completely off guard.

"That's all you have to say?" I reply, incredulously.

"I dunno. You both could do a whole helluva lot worse."

"I thought you'd freak out, man. The last time this subject came up you threatened to beat my ass. Actually, if memory serves me right, you did beat my ass," I argue.

"Yeah, I did. But only because you let me. Considering I had the testosterone of a seventeen-year-old coursing through my veins, and my sister's bone was poking out of her arm, what else did you expect to happen?"

A wave of guilt crashes into me. "That was a horrible day. The worst."

"It was, but it was also a long time ago. And once I got over the initial shock and anger, I realized it wasn't your fault. Shit happens."

"Yeah, but I can understand why you wouldn't want me near your sister."

He sighs long and hard. "Two of the people I care most about in this world getting together? It would be a relief, actually. After all, I know what kind of guy you are, and that you'd never do anything to intentionally hurt her."

My mind veers back to the accident, and Roxy sobbing on the arena floor. How Milton can say this boggles my mind. Even crazier is the fact he sounds like he means it.

He continues, "Don't get me wrong. I want you to spare me the fucking details for sure. Everything about your relationship will be TMI to me. But my sister's a grown-ass woman, and she's basically had a crush on you since forever. So, I guess all I'm really saying is try not to break her heart or get your own heart broken. And whatever you do, don't let her fall off another horse."

I wince, saying, "It's still too soon for that joke, man."

"It's been thirteen years..."

"Yeah, but still—"

He cuts me off. "She still loves wildflowers, especially larkspur and brittle bush, and I'll feel a whole lot better about her on the rez with you around. They're not always the safest places for women, after all. She'll probably start nagging you to grow your hair out. But you already know that. If you can put up with all that shit, you should be good."

"Wait, what are you saying, Milton?"

"That you have my fucking blessing or whatever it is that motivated this call. I don't know why all of this surprises you. You're already family, after all."

His words stun me into silence. I've needed to hear this from him for years now, and I didn't even know it. Maybe that's what family is...a group of people bound together by love no matter what. Even when they're punching mad at each other. Even when silence and distance feel like the only course of action.

"You don't know how much that means to me, Milt," I manage, trying hard to steel the emotion in my voice.

"I probably don't say that enough. You've always been like a brother to me, and I'd say the same for Roxy. But that'd be fucking weird considering the rest of this conversation."

I chuckle. *Could Roxy and I make each other happy?* I rub the spot over my heart where a strange warmth grows with each thought of a shared future with her. The future I haven't dared let myself imagine since high school.

"Oh, and Hawk, this probably goes without saying. But you and I both know you had some pretty tough demons you were struggling with towards the end of service. You did a lot of therapy to work through them. But you're going to have to clue Roxy in on at least some of it..."

"She doesn't have the security clearance for most of it," I sigh, flooded with a tangle of emotions too strange to untie, let alone analyze.

"I get it. But what you can tell her, you should. Don't worry. Roxy may gossip a blue streak, but anything you say in strict confidence, she'll keep. And she's very understanding when it comes to stuff us soldiers face."

"Got it," I reply, feeling my stomach drop. *Am I really fucking considering this?* "You know, I called you to beat some sense into my head, Milt. I wasn't expecting this."

He laughs deep in his throat. "Well, I've been anticipating this conversation for years now, bro, and as much as I'd like to give you a hard time, I know nobody will protect and care for my little sister better than you. But I'm always up for kicking your ass next time I'm on leave, if it makes you feel any better."

Chapter Five

ROXY

I stand in front of the dark green door to Turner's palatial cabin feeling the hostility pouring through the peep hole. To my surprise, the door squeaks open, and Lily frowns at me, turning and walking away, although she leaves the door open for me to follow her.

The house is quiet except for the padding of the redhead's stockinged feet and the sound of her silver Weimaraner Trix's nails clicking on the wood floor.

I observe, "You know, they say a dog's nails are too long if you can hear them tapping on the floor when they walk."

She shrugs, still not turning around to face me. I've become the unofficial surrogate mom to many of the stray cats and dogs that show up on Three Nations Reservation. I have a theory that people drop their unwanted pets on our land, too lazy or guilty to go to the Humane Society in Ophir City. Whatever the reason, they end up at my doorstep where I leave out extra food and water.

When I can, I capture them and take them to the local veterinarian to be spayed or neutered. I don't know how much my efforts have ultimately helped with the feral dog and cat populations, but they have won me teasing from Milt and Hawk. Apparently, you're "too rez" if you attempt to domesticate and name every animal that crosses your path.

Besides befriending and feeding these unwanted animals, I also groom and care for them. In fact, getting dogs to let me trim their nails is more or less a side hobby of mine, at this point. "You know, if you have some clippers lying around, I can do his nails for you."

My offer forces Lily to turn around, her face closed off and haughty with anger. The corners of her mouth turn down as she sashays past me to the hallway closet, searching for clippers. In an area that she and Turner must've designated for Trix, she pulls out a little handheld device that looks kind of like a Dremel.

"That'll work," I say, determination steeling my voice as I take it from her. "Where do you want me to do this."

"Outside," she says, opening the slider that leads out onto Turner's massive, forested backyard. Despite the anger still radiating from her, she follows me, and we sit cross-legged on the sun-warmed concrete slab by an exterior outlet where I plug in the clippers. A half hour and countless treats later, Trix has a trim set of nails, and Lily is starting to relax and chat with me.

Apparently, the concrete slab will soon be replaced by a large, redwood deck. It sounds amazing, and she rattles on about the kids and art school in Tahoe. She even mentions her impending official marriage to Turner, though they legally tied the knot on Valentine's Day at the courthouse in Ophir City.

A marriage of convenience that sparked true love... It doesn't get more romantic than that. Jealousy pierces my thoughts, shaming me with its presence. I'd give anything to be in her shoes with Hawk. My heart still bursts remembering his invitation to the wedding and the incredible foot massage he gave me.

But after what I did, and how he rushed out of the diner, I imagine the invitation's been rescinded. Nevertheless, I promised Hawk I would deliver this apology.

Taking a deep breath, I begin, "Lily, I wanted to apologize for the trouble I caused between you and Turner. I didn't mean to. I was just looking out for your best interests. Or at least, I thought I was, but I made a mess of everything."

She presses her generous pink lips firmly together, her eyes narrowing. "You nearly broke us up."

"Yeah, that's what Hawk told me. I should've thought through my words better and not jumped to so many conclusions...especially since I've basically known your husband and his brothers my whole life. But I have a way of letting my imagination get the better of me sometimes. I'm working hard to change my ways, though."

Case in point...not reading anything more into Hawk's wedding invitation beyond the fact he wants Lily and I to get along.

"Do you have a thing for Turner?" she asks, lifting her chin defiantly. "I need to know."

I chuckle, shaking my head. *Why does everyone think this?* "No offense. Your husband's a good-looking guy. But he's not really my type. Besides..."

"Besides what?"

I shake my head. I've already said too much.

She raises an eyebrow, her emerald green eyes searching my face.

I let out a sigh. Realizing I have to prove I don't have a thing for Turner, my shoulders hunch forward in resignation. "You have to promise you won't tell anyone."

"I promise," she says, scrutinizing my face.

"I've had a thing for Hawk for as long as I can remember,"

I confess, looking down at my black tank top and flowing olive-colored skirt. I finger the black lace edge of my shirt distractedly. "Of course, it's a one-sided thing."

Silence sits between us until my curiosity can't take it anymore, and I have to look up. Her face is awash in surprise. "Are you so sure it's one-sided?"

I nod firmly. *Pretty damn sure after this morning.*

Her frown deepens, and she looks less than convinced. "He's a great guy. I can see why you'd like him."

"Along with most of the women in Hollister…"

She knits her brows, pressing her lips firmly together as if she's holding back.

I continue, "He'll never run out of an entourage of skinny, blonde fan girls… Which more or less makes him a lost cause."

"Have you discussed your feelings with him?"

Does massaging his cock and balls with my foot count? I let out a strangled laugh. "Discussed my feelings? That would pretty much kill me. He's my brother's best friend, so I'd never, ever hear the end of it. I mean, they would tease me ruthlessly forever."

"Really?" Her eyebrows shoot up.

"They've teased me my whole life, if that's any indication. Besides, you've been a part of the family long enough to see what kind of girls Hawk brings around…"

She shrugs. "We haven't really had any big family gatherings yet, apart from Sunday brunches, which Hawk attends alone. All I know is being with Turner has taught me the importance of clear communication. I mean, take our situation. Yes, you told me some concerning things about my husband and his possible intentions. But I should have communicated those allegations to him and sorted them out calmly. Instead, I got super angry and exploded on him. That did more to nearly break us up than anything you told me."

Her confession shocks me, and I raise my eyebrow. "Okay, so you realize all of that, and you're still mad at me?"

Lily's face freezes, like a deer in headlights. Nodding tentatively, she replies, "Because I thought you wanted Turner, and I was pretty damn sure that's what motivated you in the first place."

I shake my head firmly.

"You were always talking about how handsome he is..." she adds, looking down. "And as a Scorpio, I hold grudges... even when it doesn't make sense."

I add, "It's in your nature." I may not have known the redhead long, but she pretty much chalks everything up to astrology.

Lily ignores my last comment, saying, "If there's anything that can be learned from what happened between Turner and me, it's the importance of airing things out *before they become a problem*. So, if you think there's any chance you want a relationship with Hawk, you need to spill it, Roxy. Besides he's no longer the little boy you grew up with. He's a seasoned military veteran who won't make fun of you for voicing your feelings, whether they're reciprocated or not."

I scowl, working hard to squash the silly hope her words instill in me. *Stop it this instant, Roxy!* All he sees you as is Nammichi. Little sister.

I let out a long sigh, realizing there's something else we need to discuss. "What are your feelings about me attending your wedding? Be honest with me, please."

Chapter Six
ROXY

ily's eyes round, and her freckled cheeks stain red. "I'm sorry I haven't sent you a save the date. Turner wanted me to. But honestly, I was really pissed at you...even though I guess I can see where you were coming from now."

"No guys want girls like us, Lily," I butt in, my voice filled with too much passion to control. "Well, at least girls like me. Obviously, Turner can't get enough of you, and I can see why. Your hair and eyes are gorgeous, and you've got a fiery personality men love. But I'm too fat and unsophisticated for anyone. All I'll ever be to Hawk is the little sister he never wanted."

Lily shakes her head, opening her mouth to speak. But I cut her off.

"Still, he invited me to be his plus-one at your wedding. At least, I think that's what he meant... It's probably just to help smooth things over, but I'd like to enjoy my one moment with him...even if it is for the wrong reasons. That said, I'll turn him down if it's going to ruin your wedding or make you feel uncomfortable in any way." *If he still wants anything to do with me after the foot...*

The redhead's face relaxes, and she leans forward to hug me. Her gesture catches me so off guard that I burst into tears before I can catch myself. In an instant, she clasps me tightly, rubbing my back. Whispering soothing words in my ear, she reassures, "Of course I want you at my wedding, Roxy. And I want you as my friend, too."

Fighting through tears, I apologize, "I'm so sorry. I didn't mean to come over here and do this to you. It's just I feel terrible about how I almost messed up your relationship with Turner. And I feel even worse about how jealous I am over the whole thing. Not because I have a crush on your husband but because I wish I had a man that loved me even half as much as Turner loves you."

She continues holding me until my sobs dissipate. I can't help but notice the delicious fragrance of fresh strawberries in her hair. Whatever shampoo she uses smells incredible.

I continue, "And the worst of it is Hawk showed up today at the Silver Fork. And we had the weirdest encounter ever. I mean, he gave me his full attention for once in his life, and he massaged my feet, and he served food for me so that I could enjoy an actual break. It was beyond bizarre. It was probably all in an effort to reconcile you and me. But it felt so amazing, and I could really get used to it...if I wasn't so unattractive and chunky."

Lily scolds, "Why do you keep saying such nasty things about yourself? You're a gorgeous woman, and you've got a great body. I don't even know what you're talking about. You might think you know what men like, but that doesn't mean it's the God's honest truth. All I can do is speak from experience, but Turner adores my curves. And you said it yourself. Before me, all my husband dated were skinny minis who hang out at the gym. What makes you think it would be any different with you and Hawk?"

"Please don't talk this way," I plead, sitting back and

swiping my hands over my face to get rid of the tear streaks on my cheeks. "I've spent years fantasizing about being with him. Only to see him continue to pick the wrong type of girl over and over again. Rail-thin, petite blondes with perfect nails, perfect hair, perfect eyelashes, and no heart or personality. I don't have the body to compete with them or the money. The last thing I need right now is false hope, because I'll never be perfect like them."

"That's the type of girl who gravitates towards him. But as far as I can tell, he's pretty shy and quiet. I can't imagine him making the first move..."

"Never," I laugh. "Women mob him. He never has to work hard to get them." I know this from things my brother has said in passing.

"Which means we don't really know what kind of woman he'd go for... As far as I can tell, none of these blonde, perfect women have been perfect for him. Am I wrong?"

I nod, fighting the urge to hope for more with Hawk. But Lily does have a point. "Maybe he invited you to the wedding to patch things up between you and me. Or maybe he did it because he's ready to try something new and different. I can't pretend to know what's going on in his head. After all, he's really quiet. But he did invite you to the wedding, and I want you to come. The last thing you need is to tear yourself down about it and assume the worst. Ninety-nine percent of success in life starts with confidence. You could use a whole lot more of it. Instead of tearing yourself down, why don't you try building yourself up and see what happens? After all, men are suckers for a confident woman."

I sit up a little straighter, contemplating her words. "I've been trying. You know, listening to self-help books about embodying leading lady energy...saying affirmations and journaling. I have so many negative thought patterns in my head.

Things I heard at school or from my grandmother. It's tough to rewire my thought patterns, but I'm working on it."

"Leading lady energy?" Lily looks confused.

"You know, instead of acting like a side character in my own life."

She nods. "That makes sense. You only get one life, after all."

"I used to be a leading lady," I venture. "In fact, Hawk and I used to rescue race together. They also call it buddy pickup. Do you know what I'm talking about?"

Lily shakes her head, so I dive into a quick explanation.

Right before her eyes glaze over, I conclude "Back then, nothing scared me. But then my freshman year of high school, I started my period for the first time, and my body began morphing in all of these crazy ways that I hoped Hawk wouldn't notice. He couldn't figure out why I suddenly wanted to quit racing. How do you tell your brother's best friend—who you've been crushing on for years—that your boobs and hips are getting in the way of competition?"

Lily laughs. "That's such an awkward stage. I would never want to go back there. But then you hit your twenties and realize you absolutely want your boobs and hips to get in the way."

"You have a point," I laugh. "Now, I've got a completely different problem. I don't know how to get him to see me as more than a little sister."

She nods, understanding flooding her face. "Well, you can start by making your wedding date with Hawk as amazing as possible."

Tears fill my eyes again, blurring Lily's form in front of me. "I came over here to patch things up with you," I splutter. "And instead you're giving me a pep talk. I'm lousy at apologizing, aren't I?"

She pulls me into her arms again, hugging me fiercely.

"The best part of your apology was clipping Trix's nails. That's a task I've been putting off for far too long, so thank you. And as for our talk, I now have a much better sense of where you were coming from when you warned me about Turner. And while I think your feelings are unfounded, especially when it comes to your scrumptious body, I do understand why you were worried about me. You've got a negative body perception. It's hard not to the way everything's geared in our consumer society. But today that's changing..."

"What do you mean?" I ask, my eyes rounding.

"I would love a reason to get out of these icky house clothes." She looks down disparagingly at her gray jogging pants and black tank top. "What do you say we head into Ophir City together to shop for a dress for you to wear to the wedding? And maybe some other leading lady clothes, too?"

"Really?" I ask, delight lighting me up from the inside out.

"It's a deal, then. Let me slip into something more presentable. I'll call Turner to make sure he's home early to watch the kids, and then we'll head out. In the meantime, feel free to help yourself to coffee."

Chapter Seven

HAWK

After the call with Milton, I drive in silence, trying to sort out my thoughts. I've loved Roxy for as long as I can remember. That's fact. But I'm starting to question the nature of that love, and whether it fits neatly into the platonic mold I've worked so hard to shove it into over the years. My hands-free device rings, and I answer it with a push of the button on my steering wheel.

"You ready to boogie, bro?" Logan's rich voice comes over the line. Another of my foster brothers, he heads up Sierra Search and Rescue, one of the only full-time search and rescue units in the Sierra Nevada Mountains.

"We've got a couple of hikers in Desolation Wilderness in need of assistance. One is a Caucasian male, mid-forties, complaining of chest pain. You good to fly?"

I run my hand over my face, still catching the smell of Roxy's honeysuckle lotion. *Fuck, you've got it bad when you like the smell of her damn feet.* I push the less than helpful thought from my mind. I'll have to deal with all this shit later.

Now, it's time to get on top of my game and back to saving

lives. "I can be to the pad in fifteen minutes. That work for you?"

"It'll have to. See you there."

"Roger that," I finish, hanging up the call.

An hour later, the bird sails above the bare, rocky ridges of Desolation Wilderness, punctuated occasionally by windswept evergreens contorted and twisted by the wind. My eyes scan the horizon, looking for a decent place to put her down.

"What about there?" Logan asks, pointing ahead.

"No, thank you. I'm hoping to avoid a one-skid land if at all possible." By one skid, I mean landing the helicopter by balancing on one of its two skids. I've done it many times in the past, and I also performed plenty of pinnacle landings while on active duty, with only the back tires of the helicopter touching the ground. But these makeshift landings are never my favorite. Hovering low to the ground, I finally find a decent spot, bringing the craft down on an area of sloping rocks at a perfect ten degree angle, the maximum this baby can safely withstand.

Logan and his crew pile out, making contact half a football field away with a concerned hiker standing over a reclining form. They work to stabilize the patient, and Logan radios over to me every now again, providing updates.

Thankfully, the patient is conscious and responsive although still complaining of chest pain. After stabilizing him, they head my direction with the stretcher.

Logan ducks into the bird for a moment, and I ask, "How are things?"

"All vitals look good. I'm starting to think this is the most expensive case of acid reflux we've ever seen. But we'll transport him to Ophir City Hospital, just in case."

I nod. "I'd like to split before this wind kicks up any further."

"So, hurry the fuck up?" My foster brother says with a

shit-eating grin. He's muscular and built like a football player with black hair and a black beard and would rather be hanging off the side of a cliff or a hoist, rescuing mountain climbers in distress. But not all search and rescue work can be so death defying.

I don't know many adrenaline junkies more extreme than he is, which is ironic considering his woman hates heights. With what she's been through, though, she has every right to never want to see another cliff. Logan had to rescue her from one a couple of years ago, and she doesn't like any reminders of that nail-biting experience.

I flew the helicopter that night and I'll never forget the improbable break of trees that held her mere inches from plunging over one of Rough & Ready's most dangerous drops. Nobody knows better than Logan and I just how unforgiving Mother Nature can be. And I don't feel like having the wind remind me of it today.

I reply, "The sooner we can get this show on the road, the better." It's always gusty above the tree line. But I'd like to lift off before the late afternoon wind becomes flight prohibitive, just in case our patient's persistent chest pains turn out to be more than Prilosec can tackle.

"Roger that," Logan replies, working efficiently and quickly with the rest of the flight crew to package, stabilize, and prepare him for transport.

"Are we able to bring his husband, too?" Logan shouts my direction, pointing his thumb over his shoulder towards the hiker's salt-and-pepper-haired companion. I nod, thankful we're working with a bare bones crew at the moment. Other-wise, the spouse would be left to his own devices for descent.

Once I've got the all-clear, we head skyward, enveloped in the majestic beauty of one of the Sierra Nevada's most remote wilderness areas. Fluffy white clouds fill the cerulean sky, already growing wispy and thin in the increasing afternoon winds. Their white forms starkly contrast with the towering granite peaks below, dappled in verdant evergreens at their lower elevations.

Occasional lakes sparkle and shimmer below us, like sapphire gems, interspersed with stubborn patches of snow, which refuse to melt despite the insistence of March's increasingly warm temperatures.

My breath catches in my throat as I take in the stunning scenery, devouring the bird's eye view flying a helicopter affords. I wonder what Roxy would think of this. Dammit, I've got to get thoughts of that woman out of my head.

Suddenly, I feel a strong hand clamp down on my shoulder. I glance backwards, registering Logan's strained face. He doesn't need to say a thing. The patient's status has changed. I register the fluster of activity behind me as I focus on getting to the hospital landing pad as quickly as possible. There's nothing else left for us to do at this point.

Logan and I communicate back and forth, using our in-flight intercom, and my suspicions are confirmed. The patient has gone into cardiac arrest mid-flight. It's the worst case scenario. Patients are worked on and stabilized on the ground. There's only so much that can be done mid-air.

I radio into the hospital to ensure emergency staff await our arrival and get the confirmation that our foster brother, Fletcher, is working tonight. Next, I call his cell phone, filling him in on the situation. "It started out as a routine rescue with the subject complaining of chest pain. Of course, Logan checked his vitals, and everything looked good. Then, mid-air, he went into cardiac arrest."

"I'm doing rounds now, but what's your ETA?" Fletcher grumbles, sounding grumpy as usual.

"Touchdown at 1630, if all goes well."

"I'll be ready for you."

"Thanks, bro. You're the best when it comes to hearts."

"Tell that to my Mandy." He refers to his on-again, off-again fiancée of five years. *Fingers crossed that this time their breakup will stick.* I shouldn't root for a couple not to make it, but I've never met a more toxic pair. I can say with complete certainty that they truly bring out the worst in each other. But I don't tell him this. Matters of the heart are always better observed from an aerial view, and he doesn't have that luxury.

My heart races, and a somber veil shrouds the helicopter as Logan and his crew take turns administering CPR. Finally, we touch down at Ophir City Hospital. The SAR crew continues working frantically inside the aircraft, screaming orders to the hospital's receiving staff as they assist their effort.

I text Fletcher as soon as we touchdown, and the stocky, clean-cut former Army physician soon appears, barking orders to everyone. He's a gifted cardiac surgeon. If anyone can save the hiker, he's the man.

The minutes tick by with excruciating slowness as medical personnel attempt to stabilize the patient enough for a move indoors. Yet, I can see the relief in Logan's face that the sight of Fletcher brings. Logan pats him on the back, giving him a sturdy head nod.

Chapter Eight

HAWK

E ventually, hospital staff push the man's stretcher indoors, leaving the SAR team with shell-shock written all over their fallen faces. We fly in silence back to the helicopter pad behind the Gold County Sheriff's Department.

After touching down, I follow Logan into Sierra Search and Rescue. He closes the door to his office behind me before taking a seat and putting his head in his hands.

"There's nothing else you could have done," I say quietly, watching the dark side of feeling responsible for other people's lives unfold before me.

"He was fine. Fully stabilized and doing great until about midway through the flight. And then shit hit the fan," he observes, staring blankly despite the fixation of his eyes on his desk in front of him.

"That fucking sucks," I reply, leaning forward. "At least you delivered him alive to the hospital. He never would've stood a chance in Desolation Wilderness."

Logan nods, bringing his gaze up to mine. "I feel bad. All his vitals, everything looked good before departure. But that joke I made about acid reflux. Shit, that's going to stay with me."

"You've given him the best shot at survival. But if it's his time, it's his time. You can't change that."

My mind flashes back to Afghanistan, the men and women I couldn't save, and the moment I heard those exact same words. The simple phrase didn't ease the horrible burden I felt in the least, and by the look on my older brother's face now, they do little to assuage the heaviness of his dark thoughts.

"It seemed like such an easy fucking case. Maybe I missed something... You know, between you and me, I was distracted this morning. Maybe I fucked up."

I shake my head. "You did everything by the book."

"And you called Fletcher. Thank you for that, bro." Logan's eyes flood with gratitude.

"It's the only thing I could think to do."

"He couldn't be in better hands."

I add, "Just like he couldn't have been in better hands with your search and rescue crew."

Logan's face looks ambivalent. Shaking his head, he explains, "Jess found out last night that she's pregnant. Can you believe it? I was on cloud nine all morning, and a little freaked out, if I'm being honest. Please don't tell anybody about this yet. She swore me to secrecy, wanting to wait until the end of the first trimester to break the news to the family. You know, just in case..."

I nod, fully aware of the uncertainty of the first trimester.

"Now, I feel like shit. I couldn't stop thinking about my woman and our growing family. Did I fucking miss something with that rescue?"

"No, man, stop putting yourself through this. Truth be told, I was a little distracted, too. And you can blame it on me.

I made you rush because I wanted to get us out of there before the big afternoon gusts rolled in."

"You were just being a smart pilot. Anyone would have advised me the same way." He shakes his head again.

"Quit beating yourself up. For all you know, the man might have spent his entire life eating shit. He could have a clogged widow maker, just waiting to put him six feet under at the first hint of excitement. You got him to the hospital. What more could you do?"

Logan levels his gaze on me, his eyes red with emotion. "I'll never get the look in his husband's eyes out of my mind... This is the part I hate the most about this job. When a seemingly straightforward, easy case goes sideways..."

"That's life for you," I reply bitterly, looking down at my hands. "I've worked with a lot of in-flight EMS over the years, and I guarantee you, nobody else would've played this any differently." I stand up, rounding Logan's desk to give him a hug, and he rises, clamping me in a firm grip.

Logan's lost people before. It's part of the game when you work search and rescue for so many years, which makes me question why this case is hitting him so much harder than usual. My guess is it has more to do with the wonderful news he received from his woman last night.

Guys like Logan and me, guys raised to always expect the worst from life and other people don't always handle the good parts of living that well. It's like the abuse of the past won't let us enjoy the happiness of the present or future, because we're always waiting for the other shoe to drop. It's a miserable way to live, and one that risks ruining our future happiness, if we let it. Especially because those around us have trouble understanding why we can't simply be joyful and live in the moment.

I declare emphatically, "Congratulations on your news. I won't breathe a word of it to anybody until you give me the all-clear. But I'm happy for you, man. You deserve this. Don't let what happened today fuck with the joy of finding out you're going to be a dad, okay? It's the best damn news you could possibly receive, and honestly, I'm jealous. I'd give pretty much anything to be in your shoes right now."

He shoots me a guarded glare.

"I mean, with a woman other than Jess, of course."

"I know you have a thing for blondes," he barks testily.

"No, they have a thing for me."

"Is that supposed to make me feel any better?" he grumbles.

"Jess only has eyes for you. You've got nothing to worry about." His woman's level of devotion is undeniable as her gaze attests every time they're in a room together. And when they're apart, all she does is talk about him.

What man wouldn't be envious of that kind of commitment? At least on some level?

"I just hope I'll be a decent father," Logan says with a grimace. "I'm the least well-equipped person on this planet to be a dad."

"You and me both," I reply. "But Dad taught us everything we need to know. And what we don't have figured out, he's here to walk us through."

Logan nods, hugging me again and slapping me hard on the back. "You always know what to say, Hawk."

His compliment couldn't be further from the truth. But neither of us is in the mood for arguing. So, I nod firmly, telling him, "You should go home early today, if your schedule allows. Spend extra time with Jess. Reassure her and let her know how grateful you are about everything. You know, actively claim your happiness instead of letting it passively happen to you."

He nods.

"Promise me you'll leave what happened this afternoon at the office."

"I promise," the gruff mountain man says, forcing the corners of his mouth upward.

Actively claim your happiness instead of let it passively happen to you. Maybe I need to hear that as much as Logan.

I nod, glancing at my watch. I'm on call at the hospital tonight and have to head back that direction. "You need anything else from me before I split?"

Logan shakes his head.

I start toward the door of his office before stopping and turning around. Pausing, I say, "And for the record, I think I may actually have a thing for dark-haired, Wa-She-Shu girls. You know, petite and curvy with hair to their waist that they keep in pretty braids and feet that smell like honeysuckle. I've just never let myself think much about it until now."

Logan scrunches his face and scratches his head as I stride purposefully from his office. Halfway through the exterior door, I hear his voice call out after me, "Oh, you mean Roxy? It's about time."

I smile, shaking my head. *Am I the last one to figure this out?*

Of course, realization and reciprocation are two very different things. No matter how I feel about her, I need to make sure her feelings are mutual. Thinking back to the action beneath the diner table, I grin, pretty damn sure they are.

Still, as much as I long to call her from the hospital, the conversation I need to have with my childhood friend should happen in person, not over the phone. Fortunately, I've got tomorrow off, which means I can go home and sleep after my shift ends at 0700 before tracking Roxy down.

Chapter Nine

Twelve hours into the shift from hell, my lower back aches, and my feet feel like they're bleeding. The delicious sensations of Hawk's foot massage from yesterday feel like they happened a lifetime ago. So does the unfamiliar exhilaration of his attention fully focused on me.

Lily and I stayed out late shopping, which meant I had to call in a favor and have my grandpa's home health nurse, Beth, stay extra late and care for his animals. While trying on dresses in Ophir City, I kept an eye glued to my phone. Just in case Hawk called or texted.

Nothing... Of course.

Then, I got up extra early this morning to do my makeup, curl my hair, and dress up in a long, cascading black skirt with a tight-fitting floral top that Lily helped me pick out. Both pieces enhance my cleavage and curves, but what's the use if Hawk won't even stop by to see me? I should've opted for more shut-eye instead.

Coffee and dreaming about a candlelit bubble bath after work are all that get me through my shift. But who am I kidding? That's still hours away, after I check in on Grandpa, touch bases with Beth, and make sure all of the chickens, goats, and horses have been fed and watered.

By all rights, I should take at least one of his horses out for a ride. It's been too long. But tonight won't be the night. After Grandpa's, it's on to my place and caring for the assortment of stray cats and dogs I keep attracting.

Jerry needs to find more help like yesterday, because Stacey and I are at our wit's end. There's no use stating the obvious, though.

Removing my apron, I decide to fold and bring it home with me rather than leave it hanging on the hook. A good laundering would do it good. Normally, I'd ask Jerry if he needs anything else from me before leaving. But considering the current state of things, I'll never leave. Instead, I press my lips tightly together, thoughts of Hawk and his unexpected visit still swimming in my head. I let out a soft sigh. God, that man is gorgeous.

As I gather my purse and takeout box with my dinner, Jerry looks up. "Anybody at Three Nations interested in a side job?"

This question has become an end-of-the-day ritual as of late. The worry and fatigue etched in his face say it all. Shrugging, I reply flatly, "I'll keep asking around. Have a good evening, boss."

"Thanks for the extra work, sweetie, and for putting up with my shit all day."

"Anything for you, Jere," I lie, blowing him an air kiss. He's not a bad man, just severely stressed. I wonder if he's gotten any response from the flyers I posted at the high school last week. Despite a vague curiosity, I'm far too tired to go back in and ask.

I make my way to my ratty old white Nissan. It's parked next to the night server Stacey's red Touareg and Jerry's black-and-rust-colored pickup truck. The makeshift back parking lot feels oddly dead and a little spooky as I fight with the lock to open the driver side door in the dark. How may times have I told Jerry he needs to get a light and camera out here?

The battery died in my key fob a couple of months back. But I haven't had the time or money to get it fixed—despite all of the overtime tips I've collected in recent weeks.

The two-lane, forested road to Three Nations feels isolated and menacing as I embark on the thirty minute drive to Grandpa's. This has to be one of the loneliest swathes of pavement in the area and one that's not always well-maintained in the winter time. Fortunately, March has been warmer than usual with few of the freak blizzards we normally get.

I turn on the radio, flipping through channels to avoid advertisements. Why do all the channels have to run commercials at the same time? I swear...

My phone rings next to me, and I gasp in surprise before laughing. I need to take it down a notch. Glancing at the lit up cell screen on the passenger seat, I see Beth's number, and I answer it.

"Hey Roxy," her cheery voice rings over the speaker.

"Hi, how's Grandpa doing today?"

In hushed tones, she says, "A little confused this evening. But that's just the sundowner's kicking in... I've explained what that is to you before, right?"

"Basically increased confusion that happens at night?"

"Exactly," she replies. "So, I stayed as long as I could with him."

"Sorry I couldn't get there sooner. Work's been kicking my patootie lately."

Beth laughs. "I feel ya. No worries. He ate a big breakfast but wasn't so interested in lunch or dinner. Before I left I made sure he took his vitamins and meds, and his vitals looked good. Ninety-eight percent oxygen and one-twenty over eighty for his blood pressure. I set him up in front of the TV with one of his favorite movies."

"*The Terminator?*"

"You got it! He does have particular movie tastes, doesn't he?"

I chuckle. "It's either that or *Miss Congeniality*. He's got a massive crush on Sandra Bullock, although getting him to admit it is like pulling teeth."

She laughs. "I love your Grandpa. He's one of my favorite clients...even if he does get a little grumpy sometimes."

"Don't we all?" I ask, seeing my screen light up with a second call.

Oh my God, Hawk's trying to call me. My cheeks burn, and my heart races, wondering what he wants to talk about. Two encounters with him in one week is more than I can possibly imagine.

"We do!" she replies with a laugh. "I'm with another client right now, so I have to go. But tell Billy I'll see him tomorrow. And as always, if you need anything, don't hesitate to call."

Watching Hawk's number go to voicemail, I work hard to slow my breathing and keep my voice steady. "Sounds good, Beth. Have a fab night!"

"You too, sweetie."

My cellphone screen says Hawk's in the middle of leaving a voicemail. Guilt creeps over me, because I don't answer. But the last thing I need right now, after the day I've had, is Hawk lecturing me about what I did yesterday. Even worse is the thought he'll clue my brother Milton in on everything.

Only when I see the message saying the voicemail is complete do I click over to listen. The tension between my legs returns at the sound of his sexy grumble. "Roxy..." There's a long pause, which almost makes me hang up. But then I hear, "We need to talk. Am I meeting you at Grandpa Billy's or your house?"

My heart drops, and a knot of desire lodges in my throat. Shit, he's coming out to the reservation? All because of one careless swipe of my foot? I can't begin to unravel what he's thinking or feeling, even though I replay his voicemail three times. All I know is he sounds grumpy, which is normal for him, and my panties are damp by the third listen.

Locking the phone screen, I throw the device back on the passenger seat, chiding myself for inattentive driving. That's all I need is to get in an accident, thanks to a handsome cowboy.

A flash of skin draws my eyes up ahead. Then, a column of greasy black hair in a shoulder-length crop. My breath catches in my throat as I realize there's a semi-naked woman sitting beside the road in the dark. *What in the hell is going on?*

Pressing the brake, I slow to a crawl, checking the rearview mirror to make sure no one's behind me. The road is dark and desolate in both directions, apart from the topless woman. I crane my head, taking in her desperate form before stopping on the embankment. It's Shelby! The girl who started working at the Silver Fork only to vanish.

My head spins at her haunting image, illuminated by my vehicle lights. She's obviously distressed, sitting on the embankment a handful of yards from the road's pavement, her mascara-streaked face dirty, bruised, or both.

What in the hell happened to her? As quickly as the thought enters my head, my memory provides the most probable answer: Randall. Her on-again, off-again, live-in boyfriend. A trucker from New Jersey, he treats her worse than shit. At least, according to everything she's told me.

I lower the window, calling, "Shelby, what happened to you?"

Looking up, her face distorts with anguish, and she exclaims, "Roxy! What are you doing here?"

She speaks so softly, I can barely make out what she's

saying. Reflexively, I turn off the radio, hollering over the engine, "Are you okay? Get in the car."

Her eyes grow hollow, and she looks away quickly, shrugging.

Scanning her body, I see she's only wearing a bra and jeans. "Get in the car!" I command, and she shakes her head, saying something I can't hear.

Frustrated, I turn the key in the ignition, shutting off the engine. "What'd you say?"

Shelby's forlorn countenance contorts as she screams, "I said 'you shouldn't be here.'"

A boom sounds on the driver's side window, and I jump in my seat, letting out a strangled shriek. Looking up, I stare in horror at four men, surrounding my car. Before my shaking hands can twist the key in the ignition to turn over the engine, the door flies open and strong hands grab my neck and shoulder, strangling the scream lodged in my throat.

Chapter Ten

HAWK

I pace back and forth in my cabin, talking out loud as I button my shirt, "Roxy, I can't stop thinking about what happened at the diner..."

No, hell no. I rub my hand over my freshly shaven face. Despite rehearsing countless lines during the shower I stepped out of a few minutes earlier, I'm still at a loss for words. I don't even know where to begin, which is fucking bizarre, considering my track record with the ladies.

Then again, women usually come onto me. Oftentimes, a little tipsy, which means I don't have to be a great conversationalist, let alone a charmer. *But fuck all! What do I say to the woman who's had my heart pounding out of my chest since yesterday morning?*

"Roxy, you were right when you scolded me earlier about calling you little sister. I should be calling you..." My voice trails off along with my thoughts.

Baby? Honey? Sexy? Beauty? I shake my head. None of those are quite right.

I've loved her my whole life, and that's part of the problem. *How do I jump the expansive chasm between childhood friends and adult lovers without making a total ass of myself?*

Maybe I need to embrace the wisdom in her earlier gesture. Instead of going for words, I should focus on actions. The thought of her petite foot between my legs puts me in a fresh lather. I'll need another shower if I keep these thoughts up.

How do I top her sexy shot over the bow anyway?

By pulling her into my arms and tasting her mouth? Letting my hands rove over her tantalizing curves? Dropping to my knees and making her scream?

Shit, that last thought brings my dick to life. The woman has me twisted. *Does she even know this?* I adjust my jeans as more guilty thoughts take a hold of my captive mind.

Shaking my head, I say, bitterly, "You never should've started this game, Roxy. You have no idea what you've done."

But the part of me currently fixated on grabbing her ample hips and sliding my cock into her slick pussy has another idea. She knew exactly what she was doing. After all, Milt said it himself. She's a grown-ass woman. I swallow loudly, savoring the possibilities of Roxy as a grown-ass woman...

Thinking back to my conversation with Milton, I remind myself that I have his full blessing. If I treat her right and make her happy. I run my hand across my buzzed head. Honestly, there's nothing I want to do more in this world.

It starts with dressing nicely and bringing her flowers. Isn't that what people do when they're courting? As for finding the right words when I see her, what do I have to worry about? She'll do enough talking for the both of us.

Images of her tempting tongue flicking over her thick, rose-colored lips fill my mind. Dammit, I need my first taste of her more than I need air. Whatever she's done to me, whatever flip she's switched has me in the same torment I felt at eighteen.

Only now it's amplified because I know what I'm missing out on with her. I can't rest until I get more...whether it's the sound of her voice, another seductive smile and wink, a touch of her hand, or a bite of the forbidden fruit my mind fixates on.

How have I lived without her this long? Through sheer denial and idiocy. But I'm ready to make up for it...*if she'll have me*. Remembering the perfect pressure of her foot against my cock puts a smile on my lips. Such a bold and unexpected move. I loved it. And I'm pretty damn sure it means she'll have me. My heart jumps, and my body strains with pent up desire.

That said, I'd feel a whole helluva lot better if she'd return my call. Or at the very least, shoot me a text. I couldn't have made my message simpler: Billy's place or hers. All I need is a single-word response.

But she's not going to make it easy on me. I guess I should've figured that yesterday morning with how she shot up from the booth and threw a sultry look over her shoulder.

My cock presses urgently against the fly of my pants at the recollection. Damn, I'll remember that confident, flirtatious move of hers until the day I die. Now, it's time to return the favor in kind, ensuring I'm as unforgettable to her.

My heart slams against my chest. I want to love her and care for her. I want to protect her and claim her as mine. I want to make her happy, so goddamn happy she'll never think about another man. Especially not my dumbass foster brother, Turner. First things first, though. Finish dressing, buy some flowers, and figure out where the hell she is...

* * *

My mouth turns down at the edges as I roll up to Grandpa Billy's house. I don't see Roxy's car and nearly drive past. But on the off chance she's got it stashed in the garage, I veer into the driveway. Besides, I'd feel guilty being this close to Grandpa Billy without visiting.

Banging on his door for the umpteenth time, I listen intently to the rustle of activity headed my way. The old man opens the door, his face haggard and confused. The sight of how much he's aged puts an instant shot of guilt in me. I should've been better about visiting him over the years.

"Grandpa Billy!" I exclaim, and his face lights up as he steps forward, wrapping me in a bear hug. He hasn't welcomed me like this since before the accident. It makes me question how good his memory is tonight. Milt has mentioned how he gets confused sometimes. Then again, I haven't come around much over the years. So, maybe I've missed out on his friendship all this time.

"Hawk, did you bring me flowers?" he asks with a puzzled laugh.

I chuckle, feeling my cheeks warm. "Actually, these are for Roxy. Is she here by chance?"

Billy shakes his head, his dark eyes scrutinizing me. "For my granddaughter? Are you courting her?"

It's a fair enough question, but one I don't know how to answer. With a lopsided smile, I admit, "I'd like to. But I don't know if she'll have me. I've already gotten Milt's blessing, but are you okay with it?"

He nods, amusement animating the lines in his face. "I wouldn't mind seeing more of you. But good luck. My granddaughter can be quite a handful. Wa-She-shu women always are." He smiles fondly, I imagine thinking back on the wife who inspired him to settle here—Dot. She died a few years back, and Milt says Billy's never been the same.

"I'm counting on it, sir." Looking past him into the darkened house, I repeat breathlessly, "Is Roxy here?"

The old man yawns, rubbing his eyes and turning on his heel to head back inside. Impatiently, he motions with his hand for me to follow.

Inside, the lights are out, and the TV screen glows, stuck on the end credits of a movie. A TV dinner stand with a half-eaten meal sits in front of the disheveled easy chair where I'm guessing he snoozed before I started hammering on the front door.

Raising his voice, Billy hollers, "Roxy, are you here? You have an admirer."

My pulse races at the sound of her name and the thought I could be moments away from seeing her again. Holding the bouquet of white daisies and lavender roses in my hands, I sweat bullets, wondering how things will go between us. I would've brought her favorite wildflowers, but they're not in bloom yet.

No footsteps or voice responds to Billy's announcement. The house remains deadly quiet.

I rack my brain, thinking back on what Roxy's told me about her daily schedule while making small talk at the diner. Lately, she's pulled long hours at the Silver Fork. But I know she's mentioned stopping by Billy's every evening after work to check in on him and care for his animals.

"Roxy," he screams again, his face tightening with frustration.

"Looks like you fell asleep in the chair, Grandpa. You want me to help you get to bed?" I feel slightly awkward, not sure what type of help the old man might need. Still, I assist intermittently with my own foster dad, so I'm no stranger to caregiving.

Billy shakes his head. "I'm not that old, son. But thanks for the offer." I can't decide whether to believe him or not.

The house phone rings, startling me from my thoughts.

Billy shakes his head, frowning. "Damn telemarketers. No telling what they want." Shuffling in his plaid slippers into the kitchen, he grabs the receiver. "Hello."

I can't remember the last time I saw a house phone. Let alone one with a cord. As always, a visit to Three Nations Reservation feels like traveling back in time.

"No, I don't think Roxy's here. She's not answering when I call her. But here, why don't you talk to Hawk..." The wizened man hands the phone to me with an emphatic nod before doddering back to the chair in the living room. I hear the opening credits to *The Terminator*. The volume's so loud, I have to cover my free ear with my hand to catch the woman's voice on the line.

"Hi, this is Beth, Billy's home health nurse. Is Roxy there?"

"I'm wondering the same thing," I mumble. It occurs to me she has no clue who I am. "I'm Hawk, by the way. Milton's best friend."

"Yes, Roxy has mentioned you before. You're the bronc busting helicopter pilot, right?"

"Yes, ma'am. That's me."

She giggles.

What the hell does that mean?

Beth asks, "And you say Roxy isn't there?"

"Not that I can tell." I haven't cased the old man's house yet, but that gorgeous raven-haired woman is not known for being quiet. Why would she start now?

"Hmm...that's weird. I was on the phone with her less than thirty minutes ago, and she told me she was stopping by Billy's before heading home. Maybe she's out with the animals?"

"Not that I can see. Can I give her a message?"

"Yes, I forgot to mention earlier that Billy's due for a refill

73

on his Xarelto. I was hoping Roxy could request a refill online so that I can pick it up for him on the way to work tomorrow."

"I'll pass along the message. One moment...just looking for a pen. Can you repeat the name of the medication again?"

She spells it for me, and I jot it down. "Thank you, ma'am. I'll let Roxy know to send a confirmation text to you. Anything else?"

The nurse pauses for a tense moment. Finally breaking the silence, she says, "I hate to repeat myself. But it's a little strange Roxy hasn't stopped by yet."

The hairs stand up on the back of my neck as she speaks. A knot tightens in my stomach, and a heavy tension fills the room. Still, I can't read too much into these feelings. I tell myself they have more to do with the bouquet of flowers on the kitchen counter than anything going on at the house.

I grumble, as if to prove it to myself, "I'm sure she's fine. Probably stopped by the store or something. But I'll keep an eye out for her. And if you hear from her, could you please tell her to give Hawk a call?"

"Of course."

"It's urgent," I add, feeling like an idiot the moment the words leave my mouth.

"Oh no! Is everything okay?"

"Yes, ma'am," I growl. "I just really need to see her."

"Ohhh," she replies with a strange lilt in her voice I can't read. "Well, as I always tell Roxy, don't hesitate to call if you need anything. Have a wonderful night."

"You do the same."

I peek in the garage, but it's empty. Unlocking my phone, I try Roxy's number again. This time, it goes straight to voice-mail without any rings. Has she turned off her phone? Is she blocking my calls?

I can't imagine she'd work so hard to avoid me after what

transpired at the diner and the way it set my body on fire. I have to hope and assume it had a similar affect on her. But as I wait for calls and texts that never come, the uneasy feeling that gripped me on the phone with Beth creeps back in.

Striding into the living room, a thought hits me. "Grandpa, is your cell phone handy?" I remember in passing Roxy talking about getting him an iPhone and turning on location services to keep tabs on him. Only he was terrible about keeping it charged and carrying it with him, so she ended up opting for Life Alert instead.

"Cell phone?" Puzzlement flashes across his face, followed by recognition. "Yes, I'm sure I have it somewhere around here. Just never use it, because I can never get it to turn on."

I've had similar conversations with my dad about this. "You have to keep the battery charged."

"Yes, that's what Roxy says. But I never remember. Is she here? And what are you doing here?"

I shake my head, sadness slamming into me at the man's obvious confusion. He's not the Billy Harjo I remember before leaving for the Navy. "No, sir, she's not here. But I hope we can use your cell phone to find her."

"Ah, yes, cell phone. That's what we're looking for..."

A half hour and many piles of stuff later, we locate the black device buried under a mound of outdated hunting magazines. Next, the wild goose chase for his charger begins.

My pulse races as I register how much time has gone by with no sign of Roxy. Maybe I've made a mistake and should've headed to her apartment. Everything that's happened is easily explainable and my overreaction will likely make me look like a stalker. But I can't rest until I know she's safe.

Finally giving up, I excuse myself outside to use the car charger in my truck. After a few tense minutes, the screen lights up, followed by a parade of notifications, most from

Roxy and highly outdated. Fortunately, there are no locks on his account. I head straight to the "Find My..." app. After flipping to people, the location of Roxy's phone lights up, and my stomach drops. She's parked along the side of what appears to be a dirt road in the middle of the reservation, a fair distance off the highway.

"Dammit!" I exclaim as realization slams into me. The only explanation for that remote a location is she's on a date. Likely at a make-out spot with some man she hasn't told me about. After her flirtatious move yesterday and seeing her pictures on LocalMatch, I should've realized she has other guys on her radar.

Milton's words ring through my head again. *She's a grown-ass woman*, which makes her current location a bit odd as I think more about it. After all, it's not like she's a high schooler sneaking around behind Grandpa's back. She has her own house and is fully capable of bringing any man who interests her back there.

An internal battle rages as I consider my next move. If I head out there and make a damn scene, she may never forgive me. But if something else is going on...my stomach twists. I can't even contemplate that option.

Milton said I'd always protect his sister. It wasn't a question or a suggestion. It was a command I'm willing to live and die by...even if it leads to some awkwardness. Heading back inside, I let Billy know I'm going after Roxy. I offer one more time to help him get to bed, but he vehemently refuses my assistance. Then, I jump into the cab of my truck, tearing out of the driveway.

As my mind continues to turn over Roxy's location, my thoughts get darker and grimmer. Any man who has her parked in such an isolated spot can't have Roxy's best interests at heart. And if that's the case, the motherfucker won't be alive much longer.

The surge of protective violence that grips me is inexplicable. I've felt this way in war zones before but rarely stateside. I grip the steering wheel until it groans beneath my fingers, my mind churning with violent thoughts I know I'm fully capable of...

Chapter Eleven

ROXY

S econds pass. I don't know how long. But I awaken with a jolt to the sound of percussive male voices.

"Bud and Breakaway, get her tied and loaded. Shelby, grab her purse and belongings out of the Nissan and give 'em to Sicko..."

"But I thought you said we were targeting men... And all we were taking is their money," a familiar female voice pleads so softly I have to strain to hear her words.

"Shut the fuck up. Grab her shit. Give it to Sicko, and then get in the back of the truck," the same male voice commands in dark, strained tones.

Another towering man with thick black hair and equally dark eyes pulls me viciously from my Nissan, bringing me abruptly to my feet. The second, with a chestnut-colored mullet steps forward and wraps a zip tie around my wrists, squinting as he tries to thread the end through the fastening mechanism.

Remembering something I saw on the internet years ago, I pull my hands into tight fists with my palms facing down side-by-side. I need to buy a little extra room between my wrists.

A sickening whir sounds followed by a thin, sharp line of pain. Still, I might have enough space to slip a hand free later. I sigh with relief.

Suddenly, a voice shouts from behind him in a thick Hispanic accent. "Fuck no, man. Haven't you ever done this before? She'll slip her restraints if you do it that way."

The first guy steps back, looking confused, and the guy with the accent takes over, spitting at me, "Put your palms together, flat."

I don't respond, continuing to hold my hands side-by-side. He raises a hand, threatening to backhand me. "Palms together, you fucking whore. Like you're praying." My whole body shakes as I comply, and he cinches the tie so tightly, I feel the blood throbbing in my wrists and hands.

A sob from behind me breaks the silence. I recognize Shelby's voice. "Please let her go," she whimpers.

"Get in the goddamn truck now," the main male voice screams towards Shelby. "Or I'll give you something to cry about." Turning towards the men and me, he orders, "Blindfold her." In the moments before they comply, I bobble my head around, trying to take in any details that could help identify them later.

I catch glimmers of long stringy brown hair and the thick, fetid smell of body odor. The guy who almost messed up my zip tie, with the brown mullet, is caucasian and wears a white, red, and black plaid flannel shirt with a large tear in one sleeve and spots of dirt. He looks to be in his late thirties or early forties. The Hispanic has replaced the towering black-haired guy.

I heard the main guy call him Sicko. He's shorter than the white dude by about four inches, and every bit of his visible brown skin is covered in ink. His hair is clean shaven, and he wears a baseball cap, advertising "Get 'Er Done Trucking Company."

A trucking company? I can't tell if it's real or a joke. God help me. I could disappear without a trace. Never to be seen again. Just like Shelby vanished a few weeks back.

"No," Shelby screams again, her voice ragged with sobs. "She's my friend, Randall. You need to let her go."

"The fuck you say? How many times do I have to tell you not to use my real name, you dumb bitch?" The man screams enraged, stepping forward. Fists fly until the black-haired Paiute woman cowers in fear and pain. As her skinny frame writhes with sobs and trembling, I notice the navy and purple bruises lining her rib cage and arms. Her face remains a patch-work of pain from countless punishments.

Staring at me, she worries her lower lip, puffy from violence with a seamed scab in the middle. Fat tears roll down her cheeks as she whispers hopelessly. "I'm so sorry. You should have never stopped."

My mind races at the sound of duct tape. The thought of having my mouth taped shut fills me with visceral terror, making my heart stutter.

"You see this?" Randall screams, pointing at Shelby. He's got thick curly brown hair threaded with gray strands and a spotty, unkempt beard. "You open that mouth of yours again, Shelby, and this is what you'll get."

The woman slouches forward in defeat, looking away from me and refusing to make eye contact. Guilt and shame penetrate her gaze, and I watch these feelings sink into the very marrow of her being, the cells of her body, and the essence of her soul. Never have I seen a person more broken. It's a stark contrast to the woman I remember seven years ago shooting three pointers and layups like they were going out of style and high-fiving her teammates as one of our local high school basketball stars.

If they can do this to her, what can they do to me? I only have a moment to dwell on this question before a rough hand clasps the hair at the back of my head, pulling my head back viciously while the other man lets go of my arm, tying a blindfold over my eyes.

As blackness clouds my vision, I feel disoriented and confused, shaking my head wildly. In less than a quarter of an hour, I've gone from a happy, empowered woman to a frightened animal, frantic to escape her captors. But like a jackrabbit embedded with coyotes, I see no way out. I hold back violent sobs as the two men haul me somewhere, barely letting my feet touch the ground.

Lifting me up into a hollow sounding space, I hear the boom of metal as they slide me forward into a cold, metallic abyss. My hands remain immobile in front of me, feeling the smoothness of metal between my legs. It's like I'm in a paddy wagon or an empty U-Haul.

"Sit the fuck down, and stay quiet, or I'll tie your hands, too," the Hispanic voice orders.

"Okay," Shelby says, her voice contorting into a sob as booming footsteps mark the exit of the two men. Doors slam shut, and I sit in silence, shivering against the sterility of the place even as I enjoy the momentary respite from our captors.

Chapter Twelve

ROXY

My body shivers with terror, and great, soul-crushing sobs seize me. The overly tight blindfold I wear sops up the tears accompanying these cries, bound so tightly to my face that my eye sockets ache.

The fluttering in my chest soon grips my whole body, sending me into a painful panic felt in every cell and muscle of my body. I can't catch my breath and feel like I'm hyperventilating. I don't know what to do.

Turning my thoughts to my companion, I try to recall everything I know about her. Shelby Swiftwater. A member of the Cui-ui Ticutta band of Paiutes from Northern Nevada. She moved here with her mom and stepdad more than ten years ago. It was a year or so after Hawk left for the Navy.

Apart from carpooling to the Silver Fork together a couple of times, I remember her basketball playing at Three Nations High School. She remains a bit of a local legend, although I'm five years older than her and graduated before she started playing for the team.

The few times I gave her rides to work, Shelby never said

much about how she got tangled up with Randall. She described him as a trucker passing through...

Fear seizes my throat as thoughts of human trafficking enter my head. I could end up anywhere, sold from truck stop to truck stop like cattle. After all, women go missing from reservations all the time—their numbers underreported, their cases often unsolved.

More tears sting my bound eyes, and I press my lips firmly together. I hear car doors slam shut and Shelby's insistent, repressed sobs. The sound of my Nissan's engine tells me Sicko's doing what Randall ordered. Ditching my car. Reservations can be lonely, desolate places. No telling how long it'll be before somebody finds my ride. By then, I could be six feet under...or worse.

The engine of the truck roars to life, rumbling and shaking the cold, hollow compartment where we sit. The vehicle jumps forward, bouncing and bumping over the dirt of the embankment as my stomach twists and knots, and everything wobbles and moves around me.

Between sobs, I manage, "Where are they taking us, Shelby?" As I talk, I use my bound hands to pull at the blindfold covering my eyes. Several attempts later, I finally manage to pull it down onto my neck. The work is futile as my eyes strain in the unrelenting darkness of our mobile prison.

My voice echoes in the large space, and I try to imagine its dimensions in my mind. The bucking of dirt gives way to a smooth ride on pavement, and I count in my head, trying to estimate how far we've gone and in which direction.

It's no use. I'm so disoriented by everything that's happened that I feel like I could vomit. A cold sweat breaks out on my forehead, and I gulp the musty air of the truck, fighting back the bile rising in my throat.

Strained sobbing continues next to me. It's the only way I know Shelby's still breathing.

I try again, "Shelby, honey, where are they taking us?"

She swallows loudly, fighting back another sob. "It's where they're taking you. You don't want to know, Roxy. God help us, you don't want to know."

Working hard to inhale without my breath shuddering in my throat, I command, "We need to figure out how to get out of this mess. If you help me with my hands, we can come up with a plan. A way to escape or fight back..."

Silence.

We must turn off the highway again, because new bumps and shudders greet us as we bounce and slide around inside our large metal cage. "Shelby, how long have you been with these guys? What's going on? You have to talk to me."

Exhaling sharply, she screams above the truck's engine, "Randall told me he loved me. He said he wanted to marry me. That I was the woman of his dreams. I moved in with him a month ago, and everything was amazing, Roxy. It was like he was a different man. So attentive and making plans for our future. But then everything changed in an instant. He got me drunk and high..." Her voice trails off as new cries grip her.

"It's okay," I encourage quietly. "Tell me what happened."

"No, it's not okay, Roxy. He drugged me, and he forced me to sleep with one of his friends. He said it would be a one time thing. That we needed the extra money and that if I really loved him, I'd obey. Then, there was another guy and another. And soon it was every night, sometimes multiple men a night. When I tried to run away, he found me and beat the shit out of me. And he told me if I didn't obey he'd take me to Marcos."

"Marcos. Who's that?"

She stifles a breath. "Marcos is who they're taking you to, Roxy. And he's a bad, bad man. So much worse than Randall."

My stomach drops at her words and the dark desperation

of her tone. But I can't give up hope. I can't let them break me the way they've broken Shelby. If there's anything I've learned with my self-help books and affirmations, it's the power of thought to change circumstances. I have to focus on what I want—escape.

Twisting and working the zip ties on my wrists, I try to remember what the video said about getting out of them. The first trick, my captors already knew about. And the second requires a tool to break the locking mechanism as well as an extra pair of hands. I can't remember the third...

Think Roxy. Think! Instead, my mind races, fluttering with adrenaline and fear.

"You need to help me with my wrists, Shelby," I command. "And we need to figure out how we can escape."

"No," she wails, her voice shaking. "If you fight them or try to get away, they'll—"

"What? Kill me? It'd be far better than whatever it is they intend to do with me."

"No," she cries, breathing hard. "They'll torture you. Make an example of you in front of everybody. I can't stand the thought of them doing that to you, Roxy."

"There has to be a way to escape these guys. Tell me more about where we're going and what we can expect. Maybe if we think this through carefully, we can find the perfect moment to..."

"First, they'll drug you. And then, they'll rape you. A whole bunch of men will rape you. And then, they'll drug you again and repeat the process. I don't remember even half of what's happened to me since Randall changed... I just don't understand. He said he loved me. What made him do this?"

I cut in sharply, "He was love bombing you, Shelby. Getting you to let your guard down and become vulnerable to him so that he could exploit and take advantage of you."

Silence greets me, and we sit this way for several minutes

85

while the truck booms and rocks over rough-hewn, poorly maintained dirt roads. Based on the ruts and bumps in the terrain, I strain to imagine which part of the reservation we're on. Or if we've already left Three Nations, altogether.

Shelby's thin voice finally breaks the silence. "Have the police been looking for me? Are my parents on the news asking for help?"

Realization slams into me with a terrible force. While her face has been plastered in publications across Rough & Ready Country, national media coverage remains non-existent. Between the jurisdictional challenges of law enforcement on the reservation and the fact Native Americans as a whole are a minority without a strong voice, nobody cares. And nobody is coming to save us. But I can't let her know that.

Instead, I steel my voice, saying, "Your face is everywhere these days. It's only a matter of time before they find you and me."

"I hope so," she replies, her voice hollow and unconvinced.

Finally, she says, "I did something really stupid, Could get me tortured and killed if they find out..."

A chill travels down my spine at the unnatural tone of her voice as she speaks. "What'd you do?"

"When Randall ordered me to grab your purse and cell phone out of the car, I purposely dropped your phone and shoved it under the right-hand passenger seat."

My heart bursts with newfound hope. "Are you serious? You're a genius, Shelby."

"Only if Sicko didn't see it in the car. And only if the authorities are looking for you and try to track your phone."

The only person expecting to see me tonight is Grandpa Billy. If I had to put money on it, I'd wager he's already fast asleep in front of the TV. But there was that strange call from Hawk... All I can do is hope.

Shelby's voice draws me back from my spiraling thoughts.

"I wish I could have done more. But I only had a second to act. I don't want you to end up like me, Roxy. That would kill me more than anything I've been through. I can't stand the thought of watching someone else endure it. Especially someone who's always been so nice and sweet to me."

"What you did with my cell phone took bravery. You're a hero, Shelby. No matter what happens, we're going to get through this, and we're going to find a way to escape... together."

Chapter Thirteen

HAWK

"Roxy's missing." The words sound like they're spoken from outside of me.

"What do you mean, bro?" My foster brother, Christian, the sheriff of Gold County inquires on the other end of the line. I have him on speaker phone.

"I tracked her white Nissan to a secluded embankment off the main highway. I'm staring at it right now."

He clears his throat. "Where are you?"

"Three Nations."

"Fuck, you know I have no jurisdiction there. Have you reported her missing to tribal law enforcement?"

"Of course, and they won't open an investigation for another twenty-four hours. Want to make sure she's truly missing."

"Could she have been in an accident or run out of gas? Do you see any footprints indicating a direction she may have started walking?"

A vibrating noise catches my ear. Searching for its source, I lean into the passenger side of the vehicle, retrieving the noise-making device from beneath the front seat. It's Roxy's cell phone. I see new notifications listing all of my attempted calls and one from Beth currently going to voicemail. I can't unlock her phone, but it shows a full signal.

"Hey, Chris, you still there?"

"Yes, what are you seeing?"

"I just found Roxy's cell phone beneath the passenger seat. There's no way she'd leave it. I mean, she's got five bars. She could've called out if she needed help." Getting into her car, I turn the key in the ignition, and it fires right up. "And she's got more than half a tank of gas. It's like she disappeared into thin air. "

I hear his wife Cricket's voice, "Chris, what's wrong?"

My brother grumbles, "We'll have to get back to this a little later, baby. I've got Hawk on the line. Roxanne Harjo's missing." I hear shuffling and typing noises in the background. "Hold on," he narrates. "I'm just logging in."

I wait silently, my heart stuck in my throat, and my eyes glued to her cell phone.

"What's your current location again?"

"Roughly ten miles down old Toll Road by the Blackwater Ranch."

I hear more typing. Finally, he says, "There are definitely a couple of places of interest where I'd start investigating if I were you. I'll shoot some addresses your way. Obviously, it'd be best if tribal law enforcement got on top of this instead of you going vigilante, though."

I clench my jaw until I hear my teeth grinding in my head. I'm ready to punch the side of her Nissan, but I hold back, knowing I need both fists fully intact to bring maximum pain to whoever took Roxy.

"Maybe if we play it as a search and rescue case we can gain access to the reservation... Shit, I'm trying to think of ways to legally get out there. I'll put a few calls in to the appropriate authorities, see what's the best way to play this. But honestly, we may need Wolfe's help. Are you absolutely certain there's no other explanation for what may have happened to her? Because if we bring black ops into this, there's no going back."

Wolfe's another of my foster brothers, a former Army Ranger and private military contractor whose public-facing job is in security. But we've all long speculated about what he really does for a living.

"Why the hell would she leave a running car and her cell phone in the middle of nowhere? It doesn't make any sense."

"Wolfe's your man then. I've got bureaucracy bullshit tying both my hands. But as a private citizen, I'm ready to act. You just say the word. And if there's anything else you think of that I can do as sheriff, let me know."

As I talk, I follow the Nissan's tire tracks in reverse into the woods with my cell phone flashlight, searching for clues that hint at what happened. After walking a decent distance into a clearing, I tell Christian, "I see at least seven sets of footprints leading toward a fresh set of truck tire tracks that look like they interconnect with an old utility road. Shit, there was a second vehicle."

"Dammit, we could use the bird's eye view from your helicopter right about now. What were you doing out at Three Nations, anyway? I thought you avoided that place."

"It's a long story... Look, I've got to follow these tracks."

"Does that mean I'm calling Wolfe, too?"

"Yes."

"Roger that. And we'll see what kind of pull Logan may have. After all, Sierra Search and Rescue has an agreement with the reservation that might come in handy."

"Thank you, Chris."

"Hey, Hawk, whatever you do, don't go in alone, guns blazing. From everything you're describing this is a potential kidnapping, maybe with a human trafficking element. There's no telling how many are involved or how well armed they may be."

"I can't let them hurt Roxy," I say firmly, climbing into the cab of my truck. "I've got to get to her before—" I can't finish the sentence.

"I understand," Christian replies. "But you're a whole helluva lot better to Roxy alive than dead."

"I know. But if this was Cricket?"

Without hesitation, my brother replies, "I'd kill every last motherfucker who laid a hand on her. And I'd make them wish with their dying breaths that they'd never been born."

I hear Cricket's soft voice in the background. "Christian, what in the world are you talking about?"

"I'll explain later, babe," he replies flatly.

"Once a Marine, always a Marine," I say drily, knowing my veteran brother means every word he just uttered. I couldn't agree with his assessment more. "I won't do anything stupid. Let me know what you hear from Logan and Wolfe."

"Will do."

Driving slowly, I circumvent the trees, finding a route that hooks up with the fresh trail left in the dust. Several minutes in, a call lights up my hands-free setup. "Wolfe, got any updates for me?"

"Chris gave me the rundown, and I'm going to be blunt with you. There's a suspicioned cartel asset in your immediate vicinity. It's where I'd start if you really do believe Roxanne's been trafficked. I'll spare you the fucking top-secret details, but my crew has had eyes on it for a while now...ever since the missing persons case for Shelby Swift-water began."

"Shelby Swiftwater," I repeat. "Didn't she work at the Silver Fork for a minute?"

"Yes, she did. Used to carpool with Roxy." How in the

world Wolfe knows this, I can't fathom...apart from the fact Roxy's a chatty Kathy.

"You don't think these two cases could be related?"

He replies, "No fucking clue. Now go over that crime scene with me again."

I repeat everything I remember as he listens intently. Finally, he says, "Jurisdiction's gonna be a tricky mother-fucker. We can go in without it, of course. Wouldn't be the first time. And I have a secret weapon in my arsenal, just in case."

"And what's that?" I ask impatiently, my heart banging in my chest. Tribal law enforcement has yet to get back to me, and every moment that ticks by brings Roxy closer to harm. If anybody lays a hand on her. If anyone hurts her in any fucking way, they're worse than dead.

"As the director of the California Historical Society, Izzie has some pull." He's talking about his wife, and I know all of this. What does my sister-in-law's job have to do with anything? "Currently, she's knee-deep in repatriating artifacts back to the reservation's museum. Three Nations has been splashing it all over the press. I'm certain she could speed up the process, under the right circumstances. Or bring it to a screeching halt, under the wrong circumstances. You get my drift?"

"You should be a politician, Wolfe."

"No way in hell. Those people are way more devious than I'll ever be. I'm just thinking of ways to apply a little jurisdic-tional pressure. You think it'll work?"

"We can't wait long enough to find out. Roxy needs our help now."

"I get it. But no matter the mission, I always keep at least one ace up my sleeve. Consider this our bargaining chip if shit hits the fan. Now, let's just hope Logan can pull a miracle from the search and rescue side of things."

"Either way, if I locate her, I'm going in."

"Not without us, Hawk. Promise me."

Rubbing my hand over my face, I say, "I can't promise you anything. If you're so worried about me, hurry up and get your ass out here."

"Alright, let me work on things from my end. Wish you were in Hollister to fly us in. But I've got a guy."

"Who's that?"

"Remember the Afghan translator I told you about a few months back? Farzad? The one we helped get out of Kabul?"

"Mmm hmm..." I bring the truck to a near stop, squinting my eyes for another sight of the tracks. The dirt is harder packed here, and the trail has vanished.

"Besides being an excellent translator, he's a pretty damn good helicopter pilot. Trained with us and flew with the Afghan military for a couple of years before everything went to shit. You okay with him taking the bird for a spin?"

"Of course," I reply. "Anything for Roxy."

"See you shortly, bro. Don't do anything stupid. Human trafficking cartels don't play nice. But then again neither do we. Stay frosty and keep your powder dry until we rendezvous with you. I'm shooting you coordinates now."

"Roger that."

The coordinates match up with the tire tracks that continue to disappear and reappear in the rough terrain of the reservation's flatlands. As I draw closer, I ditch my truck behind a break of trees, making my way on foot towards a complex of sketchy trailers and old fencing buried in the secluded depths of rangeland where forest meets sagebrush. A handful of horses and a herd of cattle graze in front of the trailers, among them a well-built gray mustang.

Towering behind the trailers is a dilapidated freight depot from the railway line that once passed through these parts transporting gold-laden ore from the mines to the mills. The sign still hangs cock-eyed from the main door frame, reading Blackwater Junction.

I see a white box truck parked behind the trailers along with an array of other vehicles, many broken down and in various states of disrepair. Lights from the trailers indicate activity inside. I slip past the perimeter fencing, slinking towards them, desperate to ascertain Roxy's whereabouts.

Chapter Fourteen

HAWK

A sudden flurry of voices and movement makes me hunker down as I hear the whir of the box truck door slide up. My ears settle on the high-pitched sound of a female crying. Then, I hear a second woman, angrily commanding someone to stop touching her. I exhale sharply, straining my ears to confirm Roxy's voice.

Thank God.

Moving stealthily, I reposition myself, rounding the collection of well-lit trailers for a better view of the box truck. Six large male figures encircle two smaller female figures.

My pulse spikes as I make out the familiar form of Roxy with her long black hair trailing down her back. Her hands are secured in front of her with a zip tie, and she has what looks like a blindfold dangling loosely around her neck. My eyes scan her frantically, looking for signs of harm or injury.

Thankfully, I don't see any. Next to her stands a taller, thinner woman with mid-length black hair. She wears a bra and jeans, and her skeletal frame is painful to look at. Despite the bruising on her face, I recognize Shelby Stillwater. Her image has been plastered all over Rough & Ready for weeks now.

Ducking down, I relay everything to Wolfe via text, my mind racing with next steps. I'm usually the guy in the air, not on the ground, so I feel out of my element. All I know is I have to get to Roxy and ensure she's safe.

Before I can form a plan, my brother responds, "You can count on about ten more armed guys inside. Hold your position. We're en route."

"How far out?" I text, frustrated.

"Fifteen minutes. See any good spots to bring down a bird?"

"Plenty. I'll be washing manure off the skids for the next month, though."

"Glad to see you've still got your sense of humor, Hawk."

"It's about all I've got. Now, quit dillydallying and get your asses over here."

I barely press "send" when I hear a ruckus behind me. "Time to go see Marcos," a deep male voice pronounces menacingly.

Shelby cries, "No." Closing the distance between her and a man with curly brown hair and a messy beard, she grabs the front of his denim shirt, pleading with him.

He seizes her by the throat, picking her up so that her toes scramble to touch the ground, then slams her hard into the dirt. The sound is sickening. "You will do what I say, when I say it. Understand, you fucking whore?"

He kicks her hard in the side, producing a sickening, hollow sound that makes my blood curdle. Shelby screams in anguish, falling forward, and he kicks her again.

Drawing my SIG Sauer M17, a round already chambered, it takes every ounce of control not to charge into the fray and intervene. But I have to play this smart or risk losing Roxy.

"Hurry the fuck up," I say under my breath, anticipating the arrival of Wolfe and his men.

Suddenly, Roxy's voice rises above the commotion. "Leave her alone, you coward!"

The curly-haired man turns on his heels, storming her direction, and I grit my teeth, seconds away from raising hell. But a shorter, Hispanic man covered in tattoos steps in front of Roxy, shoving his finger hard into the first man's chest. "No, cabrón, this one's Marcos's. Leave her the fuck alone."

Every muscle in my body goes taut at the pronouncement that Roxy belongs to another man. And my mind descends into a violent darkness I haven't visited since war time. Broken fingers, crushed bones, smashed heads. Marcos and his men will pay for ever laying claim to my woman.

The curly-haired man lunges towards the shorter guy, shoving him in the chest. "Get the fuck out of my way, Sicko," he commands authoritatively.

A spark of rage fills Sicko's eyes as he lunges forward in return, landing his fist on the first man's jaw. "You wanna play it like that, Randall? Let's see what the fuck you're made of."

He lands a second, and the larger guy topples backward stumbling as Sicko rains down punishing hits to his face and upper body. Roxy steps back, anticipating the fight will head her direction and maneuvering to get out of the way. One of the spectators grabs her arm, wheeling her backwards to stand next to him. My blood boils with indignation as I grit my teeth, fighting hard not to confront him.

Shelby is far less lucky. Randall stumbles backwards into her, and she tries desperately to scramble out of the way before he falls atop her. Sicko follows, dragging all three figures into the scrappy fist fight.

Writing and twisting to escape Randalls' weight, Shelby crawls on all fours, breaking free of the two struggling men. And then the male spectators crowd in, commentating and cheering on the struggle. Roxy remains huddled in the circle, held in place by the guy that grabbed her arm moments before.

Suddenly, gunfire breaks out from the trailers behind. The chaos of the scene freezes mid-violence, and a tall, sinister-looking gangster covered in tattoos similar to Sicko's steps forward. "What the fuck's going on out here?"

The mouths of the men drop open, but nobody speaks. As the tall, inked man approaches the circle, the spectators draw back, letting him get a glimpse of Sicko and Randall mid-fight.

"This is better than a fucking cock fight," the tall man laughs deep in his throat. "Let's see who wins. Continue, motherfuckers."

The roar of the spectators starts again, accompanied by the laughter of the head honcho. The scene is rowdy and loud, and I watch as more men pour out of the main trailer to get in on the show.

I can wait the fifteen minutes for Wolfe's crew to arrive. But it might take longer. And there's inherent danger for Roxy, wrapped up in the center of a sting operation. In the chaos, she could get shot, or her captors might manage to escape with her, slipping away into the night.

My eyes dart from the trailers to the box truck and the horses, a plan forming in my mind. My stomach tightens. I can take advantage of the current mayhem in progress, but it's a risky move. Nevertheless, I know it will work *if* Roxy can trust me one more time.

98

Chapter Fifteen

ROXY

My eyes round as I watch the utter viciousness of Randall and Sicko's fight. I saw plenty of beatdowns as a kid going to school on the reservation. Next-level beatings that left kids with stitches, broken bones, and lifelong scars, but this is a brawl to the death.

Sicko sits astride Randall's torso hammering blow after blow to his face until it resembles ground beef. His curly hair looks unrecognizable, straight and heavy with blood. Shelby elbows back into the circle, keening at the sight of her abusive boyfriend's impending destruction.

But a moment later, Randall grabs a handful of dirt, throwing it into Sicko's face. As the man screams out, struggling to see, Randall lands three solid punches. By the third, Sicko's head lolls to the side, and he slumps over. The white man gasps and crawls to his knees, grabbing hold of Sicko's head and slamming it into the ground again and again.

I can't take anymore. Breaking the hold of the man next to me, I step out of the ring. Thankfully, he's so caught up in bloodlust that he lets me go, stepping forward to watch the sickening finale.

A roar of cheers ring out, and my stomach knots as I realize they signify Randall's victory. As the men crowd in, helping the bloodied man up and kicking at Sicko's body, I look up. In the distance I hear a pounding, like the beating of a heart or the thrum of horse hooves. In the glimmering moonlight, I make out a sight so unexpected, I blink hard, straining my eyes to take it in.

A silver mustang, his coat glistening in the moonlight, heads directly towards me, a rider hunched low on his back. I make out the unmistakeable cowboy's brown Stetson, a knot settling in my throat. The sudden surge of adrenaline refreshes my memory, and in the fleeting seconds before the horse reaches me, I remember the third way to break free from zip ties.

Grabbing the end with my teeth and cinching it as tight as possible, I raise my hands over my head, separating my elbows. Bringing them down as hard as I can onto my raised knee, the restraint breaks. Almost at the same moment, the shimmering horse, and its rider reach me, flipping around. Without a second thought, I lock arms with Hawk, bounding up behind him onto the back of the horse like we used to do as kids.

He's riding bareback, and the momentum lands me only halfway on the mount, leaving me in danger of bouncing right back off. But I dig my right leg into the horse's haunches, leveraging myself into place and wrapping my arms firmly around the cowboy's muscular core. I marvel at how familiar and right this feels, as if it was always meant to be.

Heads down and bodies pressed against the horse, we ride right back through the crowd of men, jumping over Sicko and those bent-kneed attending him, at a breakneck pace. Moments pass before the din of gasps and confused voices behind us turn to gunfire. Hawk presses the horse forward at top speed, and I hang on, more flying than riding.

The sound of a helicopter whirs overhead, and I fight the

temptation to look up, pressing my head firmly into Hawk's muscular back. The cold cast of headlights flash in front of us, and the sound of engines lets me know we're being pursued.

Hawk steers the horse expertly, leading us over terrain so rugged, I hold my breath. We jump a creek and then topple over the dizzying heights of a sheer cliff face, the horse's hooves digging into the soft sediment as we plummet down the edge followed by great clouds of dust and gravel.

By the light of the moon, I recognize the spot where we're heading, and I call out, "The caves. Head to the caves."

He nods, never looking back, and I chide myself for my silliness. Of course, he knows where to go.

More gunfire rings out behind us. It sounds like a veritable war zone, and I notice the horse is already starting to sweat into a foamy lather. It makes the grip of my legs slippery, and I nearly slide off, clinging to Hawk desperately. I always knew he was a daredevil on horseback, but he takes my breath away, riding like a fiend into the stillness of night's cover.

Bringing the horse to a sudden stop, he jumps down, and I follow behind him. Smacking the horse on the rear, he sends him racing off into the distance. Clasping my hand, he leads me through the maze of rocks and brush that I know so well until we find the well-hidden mouth of the cave we often explored as children.

Once safely inside and away from the mouth, Hawk grabs his phone, turning on the flashlight to guide our steps. We descend in silence through a series of chambers and tunnels where it would be far too easy to get lost. Fortunately, we know this cave system like the back of our hands, having spent so much of our childhood down here exploring and learning its hidden depths and secrets.

Our fast-paced breathing accompanies the escape into this secluded underground world as the roar of engines rushes past outside, and I let out a sigh of relief. Hawk's plan must have worked. They're still pursuing the horse. Besides, the cave is an endless series of clandestine spots, nooks, and crannies where we can hide indefinitely without them finding us.

I hold my breath, my heart pounding in my ears and temples. Continuing further, the comfort of this subterranean place wraps me in its comfort as if I'm climbing into the living, breathing breast of Mother Earth, seeking out her sacred comfort.

Countless generations have used this cave for shelter and safety. I feel the energy of this place pulsing through me as we continue scurrying over rocks and through narrow passages until we come to a large chamber where pictographs can be made out by the light of a fire. But there will be no flames tonight. No longer can I hear the roar of action outside, and the intimacy of the darkened place overwhelms me. Finally, Hawk stops, and I softly exhale.

Chapter Sixteen

ROXY

Hawk angles his cell phone in a recess in the wall so that its thin strand of white flashlight glimmers between us, shimmering over our faces and bodies. The next thing I know, his hands are on me in the cold stillness of the cave.

He whispers frantically, "Are you okay? Did they hurt you?" He's like a crazed man, not registering my response, as his fingers and palms slide over every inch of me, my arms, my core, my legs, searching in the darkness for signs of injury.

"I'm okay," I whisper again and again, until sobs replace my words, and he envelopes me in his warm embrace. I bury my head in his shoulder, muffling my sobs.

"God," he moans, relief coloring his voice, as he crushes me in his possessive grip. His body is tense, and I can feel him trying to communicate to me, trying to let me know his thoughts and feelings. He groans in strained tones, "I thought I lost you... I can't lose you. Ever."

"How did you know I was gone? How did you find me?"

"Your cell phone," he replies, panting, his hands still roving over my frame as if he can't believe I'm unharmed.

Instead of finding injuries, his fingertips and palms incinerate the sparks of desire always sitting between us, like lighter fluid and a match to dry kindling. The juncture at the top of my legs tightens, and I let out a sigh, heavy with need.

He continues, "I went to Grandpa Billy's tonight looking for you. Got dressed up and brought you flowers, because fuck, Roxy, I can't do it anymore."

"Do what?" I whisper, my voice stuck in my throat.

"Stay away from you."

The sound that escapes me is somewhere between a word and a moan, unintelligible but the perfect expression of everything I feel. Sweeping my hands up his shoulders and corded neck to clasp his angular cheeks, I stare raptly at his generous lips. Desire wraps around me like a coiled snake, restricting the air in my lungs. I swallow loudly, noticing his eyes, molten pools of desire, drop to my mouth, too.

Somehow the quiet of the cave intensifies, growing so thick in the air I struggle to breathe. *It's now or never.* Exhaling softly, I lean into him and the cell phone flashlight's faint illumination, standing on my tiptoes and pulling him towards me until our lips meet.

I half expect the initial feel of his flesh on mine to be strange or awkward. After all, we've known each other most of our lives. To my surprise, the warmth of his soft mouth inflames my heart, making the pulse pound behind my ribs.

Yearning crackles between us as my lips ghost over his, feather-light and teasing. Without hesitation, he draws towards me, leaning in until tremors of want shake my core. I let my mouth rove over his with increasing urgency, alternating between playful nips and flirtatious swipes of the tip of my tongue.

His lips chase mine, firm and unyielding, until he captures them possessively with a growl that comes from deep within his chest. Bringing his hand up to my neck, he ravages my mouth, sending delicious shivers of pleasure swirling through my veins and straight to my heart. They turn to waves of all-consuming fire as they travel across my skin, covering my flesh in delicious anticipation.

"I love you," he says between frantic breaths. "I've always loved you...for as long as I can remember. But tonight, when I thought I lost you, something snapped in me. I can never let you go, Roxy. Even if it's selfish of me."

"I love you, too," I reply, tears of joy pouring down my face.

"I'm not a good enough man for you," he confesses regretfully. "I've killed people...done things in combat zones you couldn't imagine in your wildest dreams. Things that still haunt me and wake me up in the middle of the night screaming and covered in sweat. I'm sorry. You could do so much better than me, but I won't let you. Because I need you more than I need air. And I've decided from now on, I'm going to be selfish as fuck when it comes to you."

Before I can speak, he sweeps his demanding tongue into my mouth, gliding his palm up to my cheek and changing the angle of my head to deepen his kiss. My head swims, my mind twirling and disappearing into the primal thrum of soul-deep thirst he awakens in me.

The insistent throbbing between my legs turns painful as my core tightens, desperate for the release only he can provide. His lips steal my breath and my heart until there's nothing I wouldn't give him. My need for him fills the expansive subterranean cavern where we hide, overflowing into the swirl of night veiling us.

There are no words, no thoughts or logic in the desperate stillness of the cave. Only silence. A silence broken by the soft rustling of flesh and clothes, our heightened breathing, and the palpable desire pulsating between us.

His hands descend to my hips, squeezing my waist and

pulling me against his masculine arousal, making my panties drip. I gasp, rocking my pelvis into him, offering myself entirely. He returns the gesture, powerfully thrusting against me.

My hands find his waistband, shaking as they unfasten his belt and unbutton the top of his jeans. The feel and sound of his zipper tighten the lust in my throat, inspiring a strangled cry of pleasure as his lips shower kisses over my neck and collarbones before dropping to my breasts.

Skillfully, he bites and teases my nipples through the fabric of my shirt and bra until they form hard peaks. Pressing my hand tightly over my lips, I fight the urge to scream, still fearful of our pursuers.

Short breaths transform into ragged pants as he fists my skirt, restlessly pulling it up over my hips. His hands grow demanding as he pushes my panties to the side. Without hesitation, he sinks a thumb into my hot wetness, moaning at what he finds.

A vague thought tugs at the back of my mind. *You need to tell him*. But I push it away, awash in irrational hunger. I won't give him any excuse to hesitate.

Running his digit back and forth along the length of my slit, I gasp sharply as pleasure tightens my core. Bringing his thumb to my clit, he circles it, arousal slick, while his other fingers tease and caress my pussy. The delicious pleasure of it makes my eyes roll back in my head. My lids flutter shut as I savor his masterful touch, trying not to hyperventilate.

My fingers clumsily tug at his jeans, bringing them down over his tight ass followed by his boxer briefs. Feeling the heat and smoothness of his erect rod, I let out a needy whimper as he guides me carefully in reverse a few steps until my back and shoulders are inches from the uneven cave wall. Covering my mouth with his again, his tongue dances with mine, claiming my mouth and my breath and letting me know what's on his mind.

"Yes," I whisper frantically. "Yes." I'm answering the question he's never asked. One pulsing in the air.

Lifting me off the ground and pressing my back against the cave wall, he parts my legs, sliding between them and into my pussy with one devastating stroke. I bite down hard on my bottom lip, rocked by the immense pleasure and pain that slam into me at his demanding entry. He claims me roughly, with an animal abandon.

Wrapping my legs around his waist, I gasp and scream silently into his firm shoulder as he thrusts into me more deeply, sending excruciating waves of pleasure from my fingers to my toes.

The discomfort is more than I expected—almost too much to bear—but I won't stop him. I can't. I've wanted him and this moment for as long as I can remember, accepting the physical torment of loving him the way I've born the emotional ache for so many years.

He freezes, his entire body going rigid as he exclaims, "Goddammit, Roxy."

But I wrap my body around him more tightly, rolling my hips towards him and panting, "Please don't stop, Hawk." Finding his mouth again, I claim him the way he's claimed me, sweeping my tongue into his velvety warmth and stoking his desire.

A furious moan escapes his lips as he sinks into me again and again, his body hard with anger and lust, straining to keep me pinned against the cave wall. His arms encircle me like steel bands, holding me so tightly against his planed chest and abs that I can barely breathe. But I don't need air, I need him.

With a muffled cry, he thrusts into me again, sending waves of pulsing heat into my body as he comes. I shudder around him, milking his violent release with my own powerful orgasm. His body melts into mine as our breathing slows and synchs, and I realize his arms and legs are shaking. Unwrapping myself from him, I follow his lead as he coaxes my body gently to the cave floor until my feet hit the earth.

Wrapping his arms around me, he buries his face in the nape of my neck. I can feel the heat from his breath, which he works to slow. His heart beats wildly in his chest, and he says in an anguished tone that makes my heart sink. "Why didn't you tell me you were a virgin? How bad did I hurt you?"

I bite my lower lip, a sharp stinging between my legs and tears sliding down my cheeks. I know I'm a bad liar, so I evade his question. "I wanted everything we did together, Hawk."

He straightens, brushing the hair off my shoulders until it cascades down my back. "I didn't think there was any way you'd be a virgin at twenty-six. The thought didn't even cross my mind. I'm so sorry."

My breath shudders as I say firmly, "I'm not sorry about any of it. And you shouldn't be, either. I've wanted this moment with you for as long as I can remember."

"Your first time should be special. Not like this."

"It was perfect, because it was you."

He rests his chin atop my head. "What the fuck am I going to do with you, Roxy? All I've ever wanted is to keep you from pain. And all I seem to do is hurt you again and again."

"Stop it," I scold, wrapping my arms around his waist and snuggling into his firm chest.

He shakes his head. "You're so fucking beautiful, and your body is mouthwatering. There's no other way to describe it. And the way you kiss and touch... How in the hell were you still a virgin?"

I shrug. "Of course, I'm good at kissing and touching. I've never let a guy go any further than that."

"Why didn't you stop me, then?"

Before I can catch myself, I confess, "Because you're the reason I could never settle for anyone else."

"Shit," he says, caught between pulling away and squeezing me to his chest. His second impulse wins. "Now, I'm even angrier at myself." He showers my face in kisses and caresses, holding me solemnly in the silence of the cave. "You deserve so much better than this."

I shake my head against his chest, listening to his familiar heartbeat. The dark of the cave breeds a timelessness that leaves me completely disoriented about how long we spend this way.

Finally, reluctantly, he pulls away, saying, "We need to find out what's going on."

Next, I hear the rustling of clothes as he zips his jeans, buttons them, and refastens his belt. A heavy silence sits between us that makes the darkness of the cave a welcome relief. But a moment later, he grabs his cellphone, staring at the screen and lighting up the space between us.

His face is hard and conflicted as he asks, "Do you want to stay here? Or are you okay to walk? I've got to get to a spot with a signal to see what's going on."

"Of course, I'm okay to walk," I reply, stepping forward despite the shaking in my legs.

He frowns. Impatiently, he takes my hand, leading me to the mouth of the cave where he gets a signal. He turns off the flashlight and turns down the glare of the screen. I assume to avoid catching the attention of those who raced us here.

The night is utterly and completely silent, except for the otherworldly sounds of distant coyotes. A pregnant fore-boding hangs in the quiet air where once the sound of engines, gunfire, and yells pierced the night.

"Is everything okay?" I whisper, wondering who he's talking to and what's going on.

He looks at me, his face rigid. "Wolfe and his men are

mopping up the scene, but they've got it more or less secured. They're sending Rutger around to pick us up."

My breath catches in my throat. "Wolfe and Rutger? What are they doing here?"

"It's a long story." His brows knit together as he gazes at me long and hard, before wrapping my hair possessively around his hand and pulling me into him for a kiss.

"We need to talk later," he says quietly. "After I'm a little less fucking furious." His face looks rueful as his lips press firmly together, and he stands up, walking towards the mouth of the cave and staring out into the moon-painted night.

"Furious at me?" I ask.

"At myself."

Gazing at the sky, the stars dance overhead like thousands of flickering crystals. I wrap my arms around myself, shivering as my teeth chatter.

He must hear the sound of my body registering the chill of night, because Hawk motions me to him. Wrapping me tightly in his arms, he croons solemnly, "I'll keep you warm." Nestling his head in my locks again, he kisses my shoulder reminding me of the excruciating ecstasy still fresh on my skin.

The distant sound of more horses' hooves pierces the night. Soon, Rutger appears below us looking oddly out of place, thanks to his paramilitary gear, on the back of a large Palomino. The blond, unshaven cowboy frequents the Silver Fork with his bride, a stunning black lounge singer named Bijou. But without his customary boots, jeans, and hat, you'd never believe he's from Sugar Land, Texas.

He calls up to us, "I didn't have time to tack them up. But Wolfe assured me you're both solid riders."

Hawk exhales, a pained look on his face. "Why didn't you snag one of their vehicles?"

"And drive it over this fucking terrain? Hell no. This is a horse-only zone."

Hawk frowns, frustration etched deeply in his brow, as he asks in low tones, "Roxy, are you good to ride? Be honest."

"Of course," I say, breezing past him and making the careful descent to the closest mare, a compact American Quarter Horse. Pulling myself up onto her back, my cheeks burn as I swallow the discomfort the move elicits. I raise my chin proudly, unwilling to admit vulnerability.

Resignation floods his face, and he scrambles down after me, jumping on the back of the third horse. An unkempt Mustang, it doesn't look especially well broken. But Hawk's got it handled. A bareback bronc buster in the rodeo ring, he masters the creature quickly, turning its rebellious raring and fussing into spirited compliance. Wordlessly, we ride into the night.

My body tightens and nausea creeps over me as we get closer to the trailers, and the box truck comes into sight. I know why we need to return. The logic and reasoning are clear. But the panic that creeps into my core feels primal, inescapable.

"Do we really have to go back?" I sob in a panic, shooting Hawk an anxious look.

"It's okay, my heart," he replies, bringing his horse next to mine and grabbing my hand. He squeezes, concern flooding his face. "Wolfe and his crew have secured the location." *My heart*. He's never called me that before. The words sound perfect on his lips.

Chapter Seventeen

HAWK

At the trailers, Wolfe and his crew preside over a line of men, lying face down in the dirt with their ankles and their hands zip tied tightly behind them. They're lined up in two rows behind the white box van in preparation for loading. I relish the thought of them getting some of their own medicine, although they deserve far worse.

Roxy spits at one group of men as she passes, cursing them in her native language. I only know a handful of Wašiw words. All told, the language is spoken fluently by less than twenty people, and Roxy isn't even one of them. But I can tell by her vindictive tone, that her intent is scathing.

Glancing over my shoulder at the woman I nearly lost, my breath catches in my throat. She's not pretty. She's stunning. Even with her hair a mess and her face dusty and streaked with tears. My mind wanders back to the cave and the frantic urgency to claim her. I don't know what came over me. I was out of my mind with need, and I'll be angry with myself forever. She deserves so much more.

Didn't I swear to Milton I'd never hurt her and always protect her? Well, I'm pretty damn sure I hurt her, even

112

though she pressed her lips firmly together, refusing to complain. *That woman.*

Even worse, I did everything wrong. We didn't talk about birth control or STDs or any of it. I've never felt more disgusted with myself, and my heart bleeds, searching for a way to make it up to her. To make things right with her. But it's too damn late for that.

Jumping down from the Mustang, I offer Roxy my hand. She takes it, dismounting fluidly with her head held high like a First Nations Princess. I'll never be a good enough man for her. But I'm too damn bad to relinquish her. Instead, I pull her into my arms, planting a firm kiss on her rosy lips.

A strong hand clasps my shoulder, and reluctantly, I pull away. Turning, I see my brother, Wolfe, taking in my interlude with Roxy. The burly Ranger looks like a professional wrestler, curiosity shrouding his paint-blackened face. At six foot six, he towers three inches above me, looking fierce as hell in black paramilitary gear.

Despite the intimidating appearance, he claps me in a bear hug, saying, "You have no fucking clue how relieved I was when we got your text. You know, you scared the shit out of Marcos and his men. Some of them swear up and down a ghost riding a phantom horse rescued Roxy."

I chuckle deep in my throat. "That's a rumor I'd be happy to perpetuate if it protects more women and girls out here."

"Speaking of that," Wolfe says gravely, his voice trailing off. "I have something to show you."

I look over my shoulder, searching for Roxy. My eyes find her, bent down and talking to Shelby. A man stands next to them with his arms crossed. He's got a bodybuilder's physique and a stern, unsmiling face. But there's a softness to the way the black-bearded man looks at Shelby that makes me wonder if they know each other.

I call towards Roxy, "Are you good if I follow Wolfe for a moment?"

She nods, her expression working hard to appear brave. All I want to do is fold her in my arms, care for her, and love her. But first, I've got to get down on my knees and beg her to forgive me for my dumbass indiscretion in the cave. And then, I've got to spend the rest of my life showing her how a man properly makes love to his woman...if she'll still have me.

Wolfe motions over his shoulder for me to follow as the burly soldier stalks towards the abandoned train depot behind the trailers. Glancing over his shoulder, he notes, "That's Farzad, by the way. I'm not saying we found your replacement, Hawk, but he handled the bird decently."

My neck cranes as I search the premises for the helicopter.

"It's behind the train depot," he observes as if reading my mind.

We walk up the rickety stairs of the ancient building. When the door opens, sobbing and speaking flood my ears. Looking around, I realize we stand amid a crowd of women and children. Some embrace and hold each other, talking frantically. Others stare off, their expressions hollow. I start counting but finally give up. They come from all races, backgrounds, and of varying ages.

My brother's face is grave as he says, "We've recovered over one hundred victims so far, trafficked through a sketchy trucking company. Tribal law enforcement, the FBI, and US Marshalls are en route. This is going to be one helluva case. We'll need statements from you and Roxy. Does she have any injuries or need medical assistance?

"No," I say, my head bobbing back and forth between Wolfe and the sea of victims. "Did you have any idea the operation tonight would lead to a sting of this magnitude?"

Wolfe scratches his head. "No, but it shouldn't surprise me. The human trafficking network is pervasive, both nationally and internationally. One of the most frustrating parts of this job is dealing with the corruption at every level of local and national government. Judges own trucking companies involved in illegal drug running and human trafficking, like this one. District attorneys won't take on cases, because they know going in, they won't win. Bankers, law enforcement, title companies, social workers... You name it, there are people involved at every damn level of this, and they're all covering each other's asses. All we can do is keep busting them until public outcry forces the upper echelons to do something about it."

"And I suppose these folks chose the reservation because of the complicated jurisdiction?"

"It can contribute to the perfect blindspot, depending on the reservation, its relationships and agreements with local law enforcement, state regulations, you catch my drift."

I nod, feeling overwhelmed as my eyes sweep the depot again.

"Alright, let's get you and Roxy's official statements so that I can let you two get out of here."

I nod, exhaustion finally creeping into my muscles and bones. Glancing at my watch, I realize in shock it's well past midnight. I turn, heading towards the depot door to find Roxy, but Wolfe's voice stops me.

He observes cooly, "By the way, when this is all over, and you've had a little time to rest up, you're going fishing with me. I want the full scoop on why I just caught you lip-locked with Milt's little sister. Does he know, by the way?"

"Sure does," I reply, unable to fight the hesitant grin that captures my face. "And I have his blessing, too. Now, I just have to convince Roxy that I'm the man for her."

"The way women throw themselves at you? That shouldn't be a problem."

"Roxy's different," I reply with a firm nod. "And she

deserves the goddamn world. I don't know if I'm the man who can give it to her, but I sure as hell am determined to figure it out."

* * *

Hours of questioning go by, and by the time we hop into my truck to leave, Roxy can barely keep her eyes open. I listen to her soft, relaxed breathing on the drive to the modest, one-bedroom home where she lives.

Rushing around to the passenger side of the cab, I open it ready to pull her into my arms and carry her to the front door. But she insists on walking. Still, she has trouble putting one foot in front of the other, and she leans on me all the way inside.

I take her into her bedroom, noting the lavender decor. It reminds me of the daisies and roses still sitting on the back seat of my truck. I make a mental note to grab them and bring them in after putting Roxy to bed.

There's not one corner of this place cut out for a man's presence. But I intend on changing that, carving out a little spot later, like I plan on carving out a piece of her heart that's all my own. And more than anything, when the time is right, I hope to convince her and Billy to move into my cabin. It's roomy and comfortable with lots of extra bedrooms I've always hoped to fill with children.

Scolding myself for getting so far ahead of things, I help Roxy out of shoes and clothes, leaving her in her bra and underwear and helping her under the covers. Striding into the bathroom, I grab a wash cloth, dousing it in warm water before heading back into the bedroom and gently washing the dirt from her face and arms.

Anger flares as I find dark spots on her arms and wrists that don't wash away, bruises from her ordeal. I clench my jaws tightly, wishing I could get my hands on some of the men involved in trying to steal my girl. I would rip them apart with my bare hands and relish every moment of it.

Softly, she says, "Please don't leave me." Her voice is so drowsy, I have to concentrate to make out the words, and her eyes remain closed. But the sentiment that she wants me here with her, protecting her, warms and expands my heart.

"I'm never leaving you again," I pledge, my voice thick with emotion. "If you'll have me."

A smile turns up the edges of her sleepy face, and she nods almost imperceptibly before her breathing relaxes into sleep. I know it's not a firm answer. But I count it as a start.

After jumping into her shower, and marveling at all of the sweet-smelling shower gels, bath soaps, shampoos, and conditioners lining the shower stall shelves, I turn out the lights, climbing into bed next to her and swallowing hard at the wonderful feel of her soft body in my arms. The flowers will have to wait until tomorrow.

She snuggles back into me, pressing her soft, round ass into my cock and pulling my arms more tightly around her. I could get used to this.

Chapter Eighteen

ROXY

I wake up with a start, the bed next to me empty and cold. Did I dream it all? My mind races as I think back over the events of yesterday...the longest damn day of my entire life.

The sting of abandonment rises from my heart to my eyes, as I wipe away the fat tear drops that immediately form. Hawk left me...after I begged him to stay. *What else did I expect?*

But then a rustling in the kitchen catches my ears. The clanging of pots and pans, and a deep voice talking. I strain hard to listen, recognizing Hawk's voice with a spike of my pulse.

Who in the world is he talking to?

"You've had enough. Back up and let the little guys have some," he scolds.

My forehead knits as I try to it figure out... Then, I laugh. He's talking to the dogs and cats that show up daily on my back porch for food and water. Sure enough, I hear the sliding door in the living room close and then the clink of plates.

Delicious odors waft towards my nostrils. Freshly ground and brewing coffee. The sweet smell of Applewood bacon and savory eggs...and something else. Something sweet like pastries or muffins.

I stretch, finally registering my physical state. My muscles ache from head to toe with a soreness I've never experienced before. I have pains in places I didn't even know I had muscles and a sensitivity between my legs that makes me smile. So, the cave wasn't a figment of my imagination, after all.

The door to the bedroom squeaks open, and the handsome Sho-Ban cowboy enters the room, the muscles of his chest and shoulders straining against his white undershirt. An ear-to-ear grin illuminates his face, as he says quietly, "You're finally awake. How are you feeling, Nam—" He stops halfway through the endearment, his face frozen in recognition. Running a hand across his buzzed head, he corrects, "I guess I should quit calling you that. You need a new title, a better one."

Sitting on the edge of the bed, he leans in, kissing me tenderly. His lips dance lightly over mine.

"I like 'my heart,'" I encourage, and he smiles.

"And I can't think of a name that better suits what you are to me."

Leaning forward, I return his kiss hungrily, drawing him into me with an urgency echoing my feelings in the cave last night.

Pulling back gently, he scolds, "Before we get ahead of ourselves, you should take a shower and get cleaned up. I tried with a washcloth last night. But I know you'll feel better after you do whatever it is you do with all those fancy-smelling soaps and shampoos."

I arch an eyebrow at him.

He chuckles, explaining, "After we got back here last night...well, I guess this morning, I hopped in the shower. Couldn't figure out which, if any of those fancy products would work on me. Fortunately, I found an old bar of soap under the sink. Hope you're okay with that?" He winks.

"I like the way you smell," I confess, feeling my cheeks darken.

"That's a good thing," he says in low, seductive tones that make my whole body feel like it's melting. Clearing his throat, he commands gruffly, "Now hurry and take a shower. I've got breakfast waiting for you."

Thirty minutes later, I feel a million times better. The heat of the shower has taken some of the sting and soreness out of my muscles, and I feel clean and happy, enveloped in the smell of honeysuckle body wash and hair care products.

I cover my mouth with my hand as I walk into the living room, spying the modest dining room table piled high with crispy bacon, scrambled eggs, and blueberry muffins. Two mugs of coffee steam. Behind the mouthwatering spread, a bouquet of daisies and lavender roses provides a splash of color.

Suddenly, responsibility crashes into me. Gasping, I exclaim, "I'm supposed to be working at the Silver Fork right now. Oh no!" My mouth hangs open, and I hesitate between sitting down at the table and running into my bedroom to change. "And what about Grandpa Billy? I have to go see him and call his nurse, Beth. And then there's Milton. He must be so worried about me."

Hawk saunters towards me, his face a tranquil sea of handsomeness. "I've already taken care of all of that. Lily's covering your shift, even though Turner's a little peeved about it. And Beth's with Grandpa right now. Milt knows what happened and that you're safe. And the animals you keep have been fed and watered. Everything's good. All you need to do is relax."

I rub my hands over my face. "I can't believe I... I can't..." Traumatic memories crash into me suddenly, still too much to process, and I burst into tears.

He closes the distance, wrapping me in his comforting arms. "It's okay, Roxy. I'm so proud of how strong you've been. But you don't have to be that way with me. You can let it all out."

His hushed words turn me into a sobbing baby, and he leads me gently to the breakfast table. Encouraging me to sit down, he kneels in front of me between my legs, still holding and comforting me until the torrent of tears slowly fades.

His hands are in my hair, gently stroking my long locks, and sending the most wonderful shivers up and down my spine. Taking a deep breath and steeling my voice, I finally get the courage to say, "You were mad last night, Hawk."

"I was," he growls, his hands going from stroking my hair to gliding over my neck and shoulders, gently but with just enough pressure to feel like a light massage. "I don't know what came over me last night. The adrenaline of almost losing you. The joy of saving you. Finally giving into the feelings I've had for you since we were in high school together. But I'm so sorry about how roughly I took your virginity. It was unacceptable, and I hope you can forgive me some day."

I bite my lower lip, staring at him through large teardrops so that his handsome face is blurred in front of me. "There's nothing to forgive you for."

"You say that now. But once you know a little more about how lovemaking works, you're going to realize how badly I fucked up our first time." I try to look away embarrassed, but he snags my chin with a finger, drawing my gaze up towards his ebony eyes. "I could've done a lot better by you last night, although it would have probably hurt no matter what. But apart from the first time, sex should feel fucking amazing for both of us."

I exhale sharply. "Thank goodness. Because that was a lot. As much as I love you, that was a lot. It had me wondering how people do it every day, let alone why they'd want to."

He sighs so close to me now that I can feel his warm breath on my cheeks. Shifting slightly, he says, "If I do my job right, you should feel exquisite. Better than amazing." He leans in, capturing my mouth with his, and I melt into him, savoring the taste of his tender, seeking mouth. The masculine authority of his claim makes my panties instantly wet, and I lean forward, ready to give him anything he wants...despite the sting of last night.

No wonder poor Shelby ended up where she did. Love is insane. It makes you feel unhinged, out of control. Thankfully, Hawk is the man Randall could never be.

"You still haven't answered my question, Roxy. Can you ever forgive me for last night?"

"It was perfect," I reply wistfully.

"No, it wasn't," he argues, shaking his head. "But when you're ready, I'll show you perfect." His hands slide down to my knees, slipping up under the silky lavender robe and nightgown I wear. Thank goodness Lily insisted I buy the set in Ophir City, along with lots of pretty, lacy underwear.

He lightly caresses the outside of my legs, taking his time and making me feel like the most precious thing on the Earth. His lips follow his fingers, tracing their way towards my inner thighs, but I stop him in a panic.

"Stop it," I say, pulling the robe over my lap.

He looks up, hurt and confused.

"My thighs are fat and gross."

He grimaces, scolding, "Don't ever talk that way again. Your thighs are mouthwatering. They're masterpieces. I want to devour every fucking inch of you. And when you're ready, I'm going to show you just how turned on your sexy body makes me. I'm going to make love to you properly, like I should have last night."

Exhaling slowly and licking my lips, I say firmly, "I'm ready."

Chapter Nineteen

ROXY

Hawk's eyes darken, narrowing. "Are you sure? The last thing I want to do is hurt you more."

"I'm ready," I say with a seductive smile. "Please, I need you now. I need you so badly."

Grabbing the back of the chair, he pulls me roughly towards him until his face is a few inches from my pussy. I can feel his hot breath on the front of my slinky lace underwear. His hands slide slowly and sensually up the sides of my legs beneath the robe, finding the waistband of my underwear and pulling them down over my legs. He tosses the flimsy lace to the floor, bringing his hands up the back side of my ass and thighs and assertively parting my legs.

"Fuck, you're beautiful," he says staring at my pussy, and lowering his head until I feel his soft, velvety tongue circle my clit for the first time. I gasp as he growls between my legs, sending sensual vibrations through my sensitive core and heightening the pressure of his tongue as he swipes back and forth through my folds. "And the way you taste is so damn good. I could eat you out like this all day."

Hawk buries his head between my legs again, and I let out

a ragged breath as his tongue flicks and teases me. I've never felt anything like this in my life. Closing my eyes, I focus on every move, every sensation, savoring the feel of his skilled hands and mouth on my flesh.

The way his tongue massages me, making me feel as if I'm dissolving into desire itself. The way his fingers get in on the action, swiping back and forth along my slick slit until I can't breathe and feel like I'm floating through the air.

His demanding hands slide over my ass, drawing me into him. My feet rest on his back as he changes his angle, diving into me with his tongue and fingers until I writhe against him, screaming his name with my tremulous release.

My legs shake and my body hums as wave after wave of tension and release wash over me. I feel my pussy clenching tightly around his finger as he uses his other hand to lightly tap my clit, making me throb and clench him with each drop of his finger.

"What was that?" I ask, breathlessly as he leans forward, wrapping his arms around me and kissing me senseless. I can taste myself on him as he devours my mouth ravenously.

"Don't play innocent with me, woman. You know exactly what that was."

"Yeah, mind-blowing."

He laughs. "I'm glad you like it, because that's how I plan on spoiling you every damn day, if you let me."

"Every day?" I gasp, still working to slow my breathing. "I like the sound of that."

He chuckles, giving me a lopsided grin. "See what I mean? A whole helluva lot better than the cave."

Shaking my head, I argue stubbornly, "Last night was perfect, too. It always will be to me, because it was our first time."

His face grows serious and his brows knot. Nodding

towards the table, he tries to change the subject, "We should probably dive into this food before it gets cold..."

"The food can wait," I say seductively. "I need to feel your cock inside of me again." My statement is only half true. But I feel the cave hanging between us like a heavy weight, one I no longer want separating us. My body belongs to him now, just like his belongs to me. I need the reassurance of his claim on me.

His jaw goes slack, and his eyes crackle with desire. "Are you sure?"

"Yes, I've never been more sure about anything."

Licking his lips slowly, he says, "There's something else we need to discuss. I should've done it last night, and I've been kicking myself all morning for my carelessness. I'm clean, and I should've used a fucking condom last night. For all we know, I might have already gotten you pregnant. You know, it only takes one time."

Biting my lower lip, I ask, "Are you scared that I might be pregnant? I would never force you to be a dad, if you didn't want to."

"And I would never force you to be a mom, if you didn't want to. For my part, I absolutely want kids. Lots of them. But I don't want to make you feel tied down if you're not ready for it."

"I want to be tied down to you, Hawk. It's all I've wanted for as long as I can remember. I'm clean, too, and I can go on birth control if you like. But I'd love to start a family with you when you're ready."

Before I can react, he jumps to his feet, sweeping me into his arms and carrying me into the bedroom. Setting me down gently on the bed, he scrambles out of his T-shirt, jeans, and underwear, as my eyes unrepentantly devour every plane and angle of his hard masculinity.

"I like it when you look at me like that," he says.

"Like what?"

"Like I belong to you." He crawls on top of me, spreading my legs gently.

"I want you to," I reply, savoring the boldness that comes with clearly voicing my desires.

Bending his head, he showers my left leg with tender kisses from my ankle to my knee. "That's a damn good thing, because I want to belong to you, too. And I want you to belong to me. Mine, and mine alone. Think you can put up with that?"

"Mine, and mine alone," I repeat, feeling my cheeks burn as I stare at his gorgeous erect cock. "Every inch of you."

He laughs bashfully, giving me a glimmer of the boy from my youth, and filling me with a tender passion that puts tears in my eyes. His lips and tongue flutter over my right leg now, eliciting tremors of delight from me as he explores the sensitive spot behind my knee.

"I want us to be family, my heart," he says, pausing and looking at me. His eyes pool, and his voice turns serious. "And when I'm not sure how to be family, I need you to show me. Because I want to do this right, more than I've ever wanted anything in my life. And I want to always know where I belong."

He leans forward, putting his hand over my heart, and tears stream down my face. I cover his hand with mine, feeling the significance of the moment. How it heals some of his childhood wounds. How it takes the sting out of the recent past that separated us only a few days ago.

"You belong with me...always," I say, firmly.

Pulling me into his arms, he ravages my mouth, stealing my breath, as his hands travel down my back, squeezing my ass and pulling me tightly against his thick rod. Catching himself, he sighs. "I'm getting ahead of myself." With a grin, he asks, "Where was I?" But I don't need to answer. He knows.

His lips travel with delirious slowness and care from my knees to my thighs, savoring every bit of flesh. Next, he teases the soft skin around my pussy with his tongue until I beg him to take me.

Sliding up my body, he guides my legs until my knees are bent on either side of him. He swipes the tip of his unyielding cock through my folds, and I tremble at his touch, exhaling loudly. Sensually and with great care, he slides in and out of me, going deeper with each thrust before pulling all the way out so that I feel every hot, glorious inch of him.

"You have to talk to me, my heart. Tell me if I'm too rough, or it hurts."

I nod, sighing in bliss as his stroke deepens. "You feel amazing inside of me... Like it's where you're supposed to be."

He caresses my face, covering me in open-mouthed kisses as the pace of his breathing intensifies, matching mine. Connection sizzles between us. I've never felt so close to another person in my entire life, and my breath catches in my throat, my eyes filling with more tears as our gazes meet.

He deepens his thrust with each pass until he's seated completely inside of me, leaving me deliciously full. Stroking my cheek gently, emotion colors his voice. "I love you."

Before I can reply, he captures my mouth, passionately drinking me in and showing me the adoration in his words. Slipping his hand between my legs, he finds my clit, circling it rapidly and skillfully until the tension between my legs is so great I feel like I'll explode.

"That's it, Roxy. I want you to come for me again. I want you to milk my cock and take everything I give you like a good girl."

"Yes," I pant, arching into him as desire shakes my core, and he captures my nipple in his mouth. I feel weightless, like I'm floating in an indescribable ecstasy as my pussy greedily clenches and relaxes, sucking him in. With a throaty scream, he comes into me, pulsing his release, and we collapse in a pile on the bed, sweaty and panting hard.

"See, what I mean?" he says, breathily. "That was way better than the cave."

I shake my head, stroking his face and chest and planting kisses where my fingertips linger. "You'll never get me to admit that. The first time was amazing. And so was this. Every time will be amazing because it'll be with you. But the first will hold a special place in my heart forever."

"Have I ever told you how stubborn you are?" he asks, flashing a handsome grin. "You can argue with me all you want, but I'll never stop blowing your mind or trying to get you to admit we can do better than the cave."

"Yes, I am stubborn. But then, so are you. That said, what's the harm in letting you try to prove me wrong?"

Epilogue
ROXY

FOUR MONTHS LATER

My eyes narrow as I stare at the paper in front of me. Nearly six thousand reports of missing indigenous women in 2016 alone with only one-hundred sixteen added to the National Missing and Unidentified Persons System.

Shaking my head, I stare at the plus-sized Native woman sitting across from me, Sylvia Blackhat. She's an independent journalist and a member of the Te-Moak band of Western Shoshone in Elko, Nevada. "Nobody's coming to save us. That's why we have to save ourselves."

Licking my lips, I nod. Nothing to argue with there. We sit in one of the familiar dark green booths at the Silver Fork. Smack dab between breakfast and lunch, the place is quiet. That's something Shelby and I both counted on when we set up this brunch date.

Hawk and his friend, Farzad, serve any customers who do straggle in. Watching these two brutish men wait tables is its own kind of eye candy. But I have to focus on this conversation.

Seated next to me, Shelby turns ashen, like she's having second thoughts. She confesses breathlessly, "I want to help. Believe me, I do. But I don't know if I'm ready to talk about what happened, yet." Her eyes fixate on the curvy thirty-something woman with perfect posture, and I can see Shelby strains not to burst into tears.

I put my hand over Shelby's, stroking it reassuringly. "You don't have to do this alone. We'll do it together."

Sylvia nods. "I've been working on this book for well over six years now, and most of my subjects can't tell their own stories. Because they're among the thousands who either remain missing or who have had their lives cut short. These women have been robbed of their voices and justice. I'm hoping this book will not only raise awareness about the Missing and Murdered Indigenous Women crisis but also provide a sense of closure and justice for their families."

"I've spent months in therapy now," Shelby continues. "Trying to sort out what happened and how I feel about it. But what I can't forgive is my part in it. Why did I gravitate towards a guy like Randall in the first place?"

Sylvia's black hair is fastened in a tight ponytail, and her ebony eyes flash, framed by long, thick lashes. Sitting back in the booth, the vinyl squeaks as her eyes narrow, and she explains, "Individuals involved in human trafficking, like Randall, are masters of identifying and exploiting others' vulnerabilities. They do this by creating dependency. Why are they so good at it? Because they make manipulating and taking advantage of others their full-time job."

Retrieving a Kleenex from her purse, Shelby dabs at her eyes. A moment later, the large muscular man serving warmups of coffee along with Hawk, appears at our table. He towers, well over six feet tall with jet black hair, a neatly trimmed ebony beard, and arresting brown-green eyes with flecks of amber.

His voice rumbles deep in his chest, dark and colored with an exotic accent, "Are you alright, Shelby?" he asks quietly.

Shelby's face beams, and her cheeks darken as she smiles at the intimidating man with a gentle voice. "Yes, Farzad. Thank you."

He was one of Wolfe's crew who helped bust Marcos's human trafficking ring. The burly man nods, his brows furrowing as concern washes over his face. "I'll be right over here if you need anything."

She nods, her eyes following him as he saunters away.

Sylvia lets out a long exhale. "Now, that's a tall drink of water. I couldn't help noticing his accent. It's very unique. Where's he from?"

"Afghanistan," Shelby whispers, her eyes straying back towards him.

Sylvia nods. "Now, that's far-flung."

I continue, relating everything Hawk has told me about the man, "Yeah, he was a translator for US forces before the withdrawal—"

Shelby cuts in, elaborating, "He's the man who saved me from Randall the night the bust went down."

"Hmm," the writer says, the corners of her mouth turning down slightly as she contemplates Shelby's words. "Well, he seems very attentive of you."

She shrugs. "After everything I've been through, I've written off relationships."

Sylvia nods. "Understandable."

I also nod. But something about the way Shelby eyes Farzad, and he boldly returns her gaze, makes me think she's not telling us everything. Glancing at my watch, I excuse, "I've really got to go. I have Lily and Turner's wedding rehearsal dinner to get to."

Grabbing my purse, I try to put some money on the table to pay for my portion of the bill, but Sylvia waves her hand. "I told you breakfast was on me. That goes for you, too, Shelby."

Both women stand up, hugging me. The writer says, "I'll be in touch soon to set up our interview."

"Are you sure you and Farzad can handle serving alone the rest of the day?" I ask Shelby, giving her one last out.

"Nope, we've got it," she says with a long sigh, staring past me at the handsome man bringing a to-go box to a patron. I can tell by the lusty look on her face there are countless ways to interpret her answer.

Hawk's arms wrap around me from behind, and he leans in whispering in my ear, "You ready, my heart?"

I nod, leaning back into him and savoring the warmth and strength of his body. He already met Sylvia this morning, so he nods to the two women appreciating his good looks before grabbing my hand and excusing us from the diner.

Thirty minutes later, we walk through the door of my house. Hawk pulls me into his arms, burying his head in the nape of my neck and hair and tenderly kissing me. A deep growl from his chest lets me know he has other things on his mind than getting ready for the rehearsal dinner.

I chuckle, wrapping my arms around him and savoring the feel of his firm, warm body. My hands rove across his muscular back, enjoying every hard plane, every well-cut muscle of his physique. "We still have so much to do," I scold. "We need to feed the animals, and take showers, and go get Grandpa Billy—"

Hawk's hands are on my ass, pulling me possessively into his full arousal. "We can multi-task when it comes to the shower, my heart. And while you're taking forever with your hair and makeup, I'll handle the animals and picking up Grandpa Billy."

I pull my head back, staring skeptically at his face. After all, Grandpa's been getting more and more forgetful.

He adds, "Beth's with him now, and she promised he'd be dressed for the rehearsal and ready to go in two hours, which gives us the perfect amount of time to shower together, get ready, and then head his direction."

"Shower together," I say on a breathless sigh, responding to Hawk's demanding hand already pressed between my legs. "That sounds amazing."

"Then, what are we waiting for?" he asks seductively, swinging me into his arms as if I weigh nothing.

Once the water's running and steam fills the bathroom, his touch grows impatient. I set a timer to make sure we don't get too far off our schedule, which makes him laugh.

Hot water runs over my face and hair as I feel him wrap his arms around me from behind. His hands fall to my hips and then the juncture between my legs. His fingers tease my slit, sliding back and forth through my warm wetness until I moan.

Through pants, I say, "I know how distracted we can get in the shower, and how long some of our recent showers have ended up taking."

"Hmm, you have a point," he says, flipping me around and covering my chest and breasts in open-mouthed kisses. He sucks one of my nipples into his mouth, and I arch into him, wrapping my arms around his neck and gasping at the delectable pleasure.

Everything about his body is unyielding, from his muscular thighs to his firm abs and his massive, erect cock. Taking his rod in my hand, I pump it as he lets out a satisfied groan. "You're getting really damn good at that, woman. It's a dangerous skill to master. At least from my point of view."

"And why's that?" I croon, massaging his engorged shaft again.

"Because there's not a fucking thing on this planet I

wouldn't do for you with my dick in your hand..." His voice trails off as I stroke his thick manhood again.

"You're lying to me now," I scold. "You've always been ready to do anything for me, whether or not I had you in my hand."

"That's right," he sighs pleasurably, shutting his eyes. "And that's because you've had my heart from the moment I met you."

"Lying again," I counter. "I was eight when we met."

I kneel in front of him, and he opens one eye, looking down in surprise as I rub my hands over his tight ass, squeezing playfully. Bringing my palms to the backs of his thighs, I lean forward, licking and teasing the tip of his gorgeous arousal. His hand finds the back of my head, adding a little pressure to encourage me.

"Fuck woman," is all he manages before I take his length in and out of my mouth, sucking and savoring his smoothness and power and the way his body responds to me.

I alternate licking and sucking his balls before returning to his granite rod until he groans with abandon. His breath comes in short pants as I bring my right hand to his balls, stroking and caressing them with my fingertips as I lick and suck him until his whole body tenses.

Suddenly, his hand goes from my head to my shoulder, stopping me. "I need your pussy," he commands, his voice dark and dangerous. "Like now."

Sliding the hand on my shoulder down my arm's full length, he grasps my fingers, pulling me up from the shower floor. Effortlessly, he hoists me into his arms, pinning me against the shower stall wall, straddling him. He sinks into me without hesitation, pumping in and out of me and stroking me with his full length.

"This reminds me of our first time," I pant, letting out a

high-pitched cry as he slams into me again, angling me against the wall to hit my G-spot perfectly.

"For the record, *this* is what I was going for," he counters through labored breaths. "But unlike the cave, now your body's actually ready for me, and I'm also better acquainted with what makes you melt." He slips a hand between my legs, circling my clit with his thumb until I see stars.

"That's it," he encourages. "I want you to come for me, and I want you to milk every drop of cum out of me. You think you can do that?"

He barely gets the question out before I scream and convulse around him, submitting fully to the bliss that rocks my core. Hawk pounds me again and again, following me over the edge with a throaty cry that makes me tremble with satisfaction. I savor the tremulous waves of heat pulsating from his body into mine. Pressing kisses on my neck and shoulders, he runs his hand through my wet tresses, breathing hard.

Beep! Beep! Beep! The alarm rudely shakes us back to reality. I'm equal parts annoyed and vindicated that I set it.

"Motherfucker," he laments, reluctantly withdrawing from me as I unclasp my arms from his neck and legs from his waist. Gently, he places me back on my feet, planting a firm kiss on my lips.

Pulling back the curtain, he leans out of the shower, straining to reach my phone on the sink counter. I wrap my arms around his hard, wet waist to keep him from falling out onto the floor. He chuckles, finally hitting the snooze button before I draw him possessively back into the stall facing me.

"We need that snooze button, you know," he observes naughtily, tracing my jaw line with his forefinger, and snagging my chin to steal another penetrating kiss. "Because I'm not even halfway through all I want to do to you."

"That's the beauty of basically living together," I remind him.

He runs both hands gently through my wet hair, letting his gaze wash over my face. "Speaking of living together. I've been thinking about it, Roxy, and I want you and Grandpa Billy to move into my cabin with me. What are your thoughts?"

My mind races. I know this is a conversation that's been on his mind for awhile now, because he's anything but subtle when it comes to hints. Thinking out loud, I say, "Since we got together, Grandpa Billy and Wyatt are now getting along again. They could definitely use each other's company. And I would love waking up next to you every single morning. But I'm going to miss the People and my dogs and cats."

"Rough & Ready Ranch is a stone's throw from Three Nations, especially on horse. I promise, I'll start attending powwows and other events with you. Just don't make me hang out in crowds too often. I've hated them since Afghanistan. And as for the cats and dogs, Maksim and I are working on something...a shelter for the rez to be run by you." Maksim is Hawk's youngest foster brother, and he owns a Husky and Malamute Rescue Shelter.

I cover my mouth with my left hand, tears welling in my eyes. "How do you know me and every one of my desires so well? Without me even asking?"

Hawk grins, grabbing my right hand and pressing it firmly palm down over his heart. I smile, feeling its strong, reassuring beat. "I've already told you. Because you're my heart now."

Beep! Beep! Beep!

"Dammit," he curses, letting go of my hand and jumping out of the shower. He dries his hand on one of the hanging towels before turning off the alarm completely.

"And we could start working on filling all those extra rooms with our babies," he hints with a brilliant smile.

"Aren't we already doing that?" I ask sweetly.

"We can do more of it. And we could think about filling that empty spot on the ring finger of your left hand..."

I gasp, and he smiles from ear-to-ear. I turn off the water, stepping out of the shower and onto the soft lavender bath rug. He grabs a dry towel, wrapping it tightly around me. "Are you saying what—"

"I'm not saying a thing until we go jewelry shopping together. But I think you get my drift." The handsome Sho-Ban cowboy winks. "Now, we better quit dilly-dallying and get ready for this wedding. I have it on good authority you'll be wearing white at the next family gathering of this magnitude."

"What's gotten into you, Hawk?" I swat at his gorgeous naked physique playfully.

He seizes me, pressing my towel-covered body tightly against his naked one. "You," he replies, his face growing serious. "You've gotten into every inch of my heart and made it yours. And you've given me something I've thirsted for my entire life—a sense of belonging and family. You've taught me what love is and shown me not only where I belong but with whom I belong. You have me body and soul, and that's never going to change. It's time to let the world know you're mine forever. My heart."

He leans down, kissing me with jealous authority. I sink into his embrace, surrounded by warmth and love, knowing I trust him with everything, and he'll never let me down.

"You're all I've wanted for as long as I can remember," I confess, running my hands over his broad shoulders. "But we're never going to make it to the dinner if we keep this up."

He sighs. "Raincheck. But only if it's a rest of our lives kind of raincheck."

"I wouldn't have it any other way," I tease, swiping my tongue playfully over his chest.

"You are so going to pay for that," he growls, running his

hands possessively through my hair and tilting my head up to claim my mouth again as the towel falls away, pooling at my ankles.

* * *

Want more from Roxy and Hawk as they build a life and family together in Rough & Ready Country?

Read the bonus scene at https://www.engrideaves.com/freebies/.

* * *

Curious to see what fate has in store for Shelby and Farzad? Read *Gifted to the Mountain Man*, part of the Log Cabin Christmas series: https://www.engrideaves.com/log-cabin-christmas/.

* * *

Army veteran and renowned cardiologist, Fletcher makes his living healing. A man of science and data, he's gifted in the operating room but incapable of mending his own deep wounds...

Until he meets Drew, a romance writer and expert in matters of the heart. Polar opposites, they couldn't approach life more differently. But fate keeps throwing them together, which has the good doctor wondering if the curvy author's capable of penning the happily ever after they both crave.

Pre-order the next steamy installment of the Rough & Ready Country series, *Love at First Beat*.

Also by Engrid Eaves

ROUGH & READY COUNTRY

Love at First Blizzard - He's a reclusive mountain man who runs a husky rescue, but his world gets turned upside down by the curvy classical musician he saves from a freak March blizzard.

Love at First Campfire - She's a headstrong, curvy true crime reporter who's never needed anybody until a handsome search and rescue unit lead risks everything to save her.

Love at First Rescue - He's a small-town sheriff who plays by the rules until his sexy dispatcher changes up the game, initiating a rescue that sets long-time passions ablaze.

Love at Second Chance - She's the new home health nurse in Rough & Ready Country, but miles of history with the grumpy ranch foreman are in danger of reigniting, despite her best intentions.

Love at First Baby - He's a wildland firefighter who refuses to settle down for anyone until the curvy hometown sweetheart and an unexpected baby make him reconsider what and who he's living for.

Love and Forgiveness - She's a museum director trying to move on until her estranged husband's security company wins her facility's contract, resurrecting long-buried passions.

Love at First Relationship - Everything about my paralegal, Jasmine, is off-limits as my much younger, inexperienced employee. But a fake relationship proposal quickly blossoms into much more.

Love at First House - A marriage of convenience is the only way to help my neighbor keep her family together. I tell myself it's a practical arrangement, but my heart has other plans.

Love at First Night - He's a helicopter pilot crushing on his best friend's little sister, Roxy. An cataclysmic night gives them a glimmer into a world of possibilities, but will love or heartbreak prevail?

Love at First Beat - Army cardiologist, Fletcher, excels at healing...
But matters of the heart are another thing. Until he meets Drew, a
romance writer, who specializes in happy endings.

Love at First Wedding

Love at First Doubt

Love at First Secret

Love at First Revenge

Love and Redemption

HUNTER'S GUILD: ELITE BOUNTY SERVICES

Possessed by the Bounty Hunter - A six-figure bounty draws me
back to my ex-fiancée and her mafia-linked Creole family. Soon, a
centuries-old curse blurs the line between hunter and hunted.

LOG CABIN CHRISTMAS

Gifted to the Mountain Man - My first Christmas stateside is
lonely until the woman I can't stop thinking about needs protection.
As sparks fly, will my cabin and my heart be big enough for two?

About the Author

Engrid Eaves publishes short, sweet, and steamy romances featuring gruff alpha male protectors and the headstrong, curvy girls they fall head over heels for.

Her heroes may have painful pasts, but they always find forever with their soulmates. Sexy, satisfying, heartfelt happily ever afters guaranteed!

If you'd like to stay in touch or get your next delicious mountain man, curvy girl romance fix (and who doesn't?), sign up for her newsletter: www.engrideaves.com.

goodreads.com/engrideaves

bookbub.com/profile/engrid-eaves

instagram.com/engrid_eaves

tiktok.com/@authorengrideaves

facebook.com/EngridEavesAuthor

www.ingramcontent.com/pod-product-compliance
Lightning Source LLC
Chambersburg PA
CBHW011435170626
46808CB00010B/3177